Edward Caswall

A May pageant and other poems

Edward Caswall

A May pageant and other poems

ISBN/EAN: 9783741185366

Manufactured in Europe, USA, Canada, Australia, Japa

Cover: Foto ©Andreas Hilbeck / pixelio.de

Manufactured and distributed by brebook publishing software
(www.brebook.com)

Edward Caswall

A May pageant and other poems

A MAY PAGEANT,

ETC.

LONDON :

ROBSON AND SON, GREAT NORTHERN PRINTING WORKS,
Pancras Road, N.W.

A MAY PAGEANT

AND

OTHER POEMS.

BY

EDWARD CASWALL,

OF THE ORATORY, BIRMINGHAM;

AUTHOR OF "LYRA CATHOLICA," ETC.

LONDON:

BURNS, LAMBERT, & CO.

PORTMAN STREET.

1865.

CONTENTS.

REGINA CŒLI, ACCIPE CORONAM,
QUAM TIBI DOMINUS PRÆPARAVIT IN ÆTERNUM.

A MAY PAGEANT.

CANTO I.

𝕿𝖍𝖊 𝖂𝖔𝖔𝖉.

IT chanced upon our great Augustin's Day,
   Late in the Holy Virgin's Month of May,
That month most mystical of all the year,
When Eden's vanish'd outlines reappear,
A Priest went forth, his Mass at sunrise said,
Upon a visit to a dying bed,
Bearing the blest Viaticum enclosed
Within the Pyx that on his breast reposed.

With eager strain upon his way he press'd,
In tender pity for a soul distress'd;
But long the road, and age, with fast and prayer,
Had stolen of his strength the better share;
And ere his failing steps had gain'd the door,
The last sad mortal agonies were o'er.

For the departed soul he stays to pray ;
The mourners solaces as best he may ;
With holy water sprinkles floor and bed ;
A holy taper sets beside the dead,
(A maiden blossom nipp'd by sudden blight,
Late of her cottage-home the joy and light) ;
Then, inly grieving o'er his labour vain,
In silence homeward turns his steps again.

In unfrequented ways the cottage stood,
Deep in the lonesome bosom of a Wood,
An ancient wood of hazel-copse and oak,
Where long had been unheard the axe's stroke ;
In broad diverging avenues disposed,
And by a belt of evergreens enclosed,
Save where, along its Western sloping side,
Sabrina's legendary waters glide ;
Still call'd (its name in early records found)
Our Lady's Wood through all the country round.
There, as he threads the grassy winding ways,
A thousand lovely objects court his gaze,
And with their new impressions woo to rest
The troublous thought that weighs upon his breast.
How softly lie empearl'd the morning dews !
Through opening vistas what enchanting views !

In what compact and orderly array
The tall young oaks their glossy stems display!
How like an azure mist from dell to dell
The hyacinths extend their gauzy veil!
Meanwhile, across the pathway, in and out,
Young rabbits gambol merrily about;
With sudden dart the blackbird skims along,
And from a further brake resumes his song;
Coos the wood-turtle from her high retreat
In concert with the lambkin's distant bleat;
And in the pleasant medley all around
Of intermingling scent and sight and sound,
Bringing such pleasant feelings in their train,
And pleasant fancies born of these again,
All Nature seems her children to invite
To general jubilation and delight.

But vainly her enticements she displays
Before the aged Priest's unconscious gaze;
He all the while for her, his child beloved,
Makes inward moan, so suddenly removed,
No Messenger of Jesus at her side!
The Sacrament of life to her denied!
Thus, as he pensively the path pursued,
At length he reach'd the middle of the Wood,

Whence all its avenues exploring went
Throughout its whole umbrageous extent,
And where, as centre of the meeting ways,
An old Druidic stone its form displays;
A venerable form, all silver'd o'er,
Abruptly rising from the turfy floor,
Whose Southern side, by droppings worn away,
Affords to pilgrims of a modern day
An elbow-chair, with fragrant moss o'erlaid
Soft as the downy growth of Tempe's shade.
Here then, for at his being's inmost source
He felt the stir of some unusual force,
And all his melting heart was running o'er
In sighs to Him whom at his breast he bore,
Upon his knees the hoary-headed Priest
Sank quickly down, and thus his Lord address'd :

" O Thou, whose hidden majesty I bear,
Forgive the fault, if mine the fault it were,
Which lost to Thy dear daughter gone to rest
At her departing hour Thy Presence blest ;
Yet well I know that she is safe with Thee,
And so Thy will be done, whate'er it be."

Thereat his Rosary the saintly man
Betwixt his fingers took, and scarce began

The beads to tell, when such a glowing flame
Of strong devotion o'er his spirit came,
That, rapt at once in ecstasy of prayer,
No more for present things he felt a care,
Earthly with heavenly seem'd blent in one,
Th' immortal in mortality begun !

Thus had he knelt, so long perchance as might
Give time some twenty Aves to recite,
When from a distant spot approaching near
A sweet and solemn chant arrests his ear ;
Confused at first, and like a tangled skein
Whose mazes to unthread we strive in vain,
But gathering into shape by slow degrees
With each fresh undulation of the breeze,
Till in a liquid cadence borne along,
Two words that seem the burden of the song
Bud forth at last, as blossom from the tree,—
" Purissima" and " Benedicite"!
Which scarce he heard, and ravish'd with the sound
In mute expectancy was gazing round,
When, lo! where in a straight perspective spread
And arbour-like uniting overhead,
An alley in the front its length displays
All golden-green beneath the crossing rays ;

At the far end he spies a glistening throng
Coming the hyacinthian floor along,
Who from the sylvan depth emerging slow,
Before his vision pass in solemn show.

Foremost a youth who more an Angel seem'd,
Upon his face such radiant beauty beam'd,
With step sedate and clear uplifted eye,
Bearing a sapphire Crucifix on high ;
Then divers minstrel boys in gold array'd,
With golden instruments whereon they play'd,
Such as on old entablatures we see,
Harp, sackbut, dulcimer, and psaltery ;
With others following, who censers bear
And swing them to the music high in air,
Diffusing such a fragrance all around
As only may in Paradise be found.
But who the Three that next in order come,
So roseate fair with Heaven's immortal bloom ?
Three Princes in Chaldea's rich attire
Walking englobed within an orb of fire !
Thro' which their face and form transfigured shine
Purg'd of terrestrial dross and made divine !
Each with a blue tiara on his head,
His sandals with imperial gems inlaid,

His wavy locks, as from asbestos spun,
Upon his ivory shoulders floating down;
His girdle mystically broider'd o'er;
Upon his hand a signet-ring of power;
While o'er his pearly-tissued raiment glow
Thousands of crosses sparkling to and fro.
Princes they seem'd, but void of princely pride,
And as they stepp'd, advancing side by side,
Forth from their lips such melody they sent,
As never mortal fancy could invent,
Which mingling with each native woodland tone,
And sweetly fusing it into its own,
So spread, and grew, and multiplied around,
Extending its circumfluence of sound,
As with an equable harmonious flood
To fill the ample circuit of the Wood.

A song it was, as nigher now reveal'd
Its voices came, a song of sacred Eld,
The Benedicite,—entoned of yore
On Dura's plain by old Euphrates' shore,
And since in Holy Church reëchoed on
The breadth of rolling centuries along;
No more array'd, as when it first was sung
In pomp of Hebrew or Chaldean tongue,

But gravely flowing forth in accents clear
Of limpíd Latin on the listening ear,
Latin, blest tongue in which the Faith is shrined,
Link of regenerated human-kind!

This, then, as leisurely they onward came,
They chanted from their amber bower of flame,
Calling in turn on all created things,
The glens, the groves, the rivulets, the springs,
The verdant fields, the variegated flowers,
Heat, frost, and dew, and fructifying showers,
Darkness and dawn, the billow and the breeze,
Mountains and hills, and all-encircling seas;
Sun, moon, and stars, in solemn order throned,
And depths of ether stretching far beyond;
On all the finny broods that roam the flood,
On all the feather'd songsters of the wood,
On all the cattle of the cultured field,
On all the roving tribes the forests yield,
On all th' angelic Ministries combined,
On all the living millions of mankind,
On all the Holy Church's royal race,
On all her holy Priests in every place,
On all the countless Spirits of the just
Waiting the resurrection from the dust,

With them in blended unity to sing
Glory and praise to all Creation's King,
Of nature as of grace the Author blest,
In trinal Personality confess'd,
Worthy of benediction o'er and o'er,
And super-exaltation evermore!

So went the hymn, upon whose concords sweet
While hung the Priest in ravishment complete,
And in a sea immersed of blind delight
Had in the listening lost all thought of sight,
The Three had pass'd; and when he look'd again,
The hinder portion of the festive train,
Like some bright phantasy of golden dawn,
Was crossing o'er the dew-bespangled lawn;
A band of youths in flowing robes array'd,
That seem'd of finely woven emerald made,
Besprent with dainty sprigs, and border'd fair
With sacred names in Grecian character;
From whence, as lightly in the breeze they wreathed,
By fits a perfume of Arabia breathed.
Each in his hand a hawthorn sceptre bore,
With tufts of richest may bestudded o'er;
Each on his brow a coronal divine
In which the fairest gifts of Spring entwine:

And ever as they tripp'd with airy tread
O'er the smooth level of the grassy glade.
Beneath their feet unwonted flow'rets sprang
Responsive to their strain, the while they sang
(At every opening left, as by intent,
From verse to verse by those who foremost
        went)
Glory to Spring's fair Queen, creation's pride,
Fairer than all created things beside,
Mother of Him from whom this mighty frame
In all its overflowing glory came;
Glory to Mary, Life's immortal Tree,
Mother of Life and Immortality!
Ere Nature yet had into being burst,
Its perfect type of beauty from the first!
More exquisite than all the gems of May;
Purer than dew, and brighter than the day;
Sweeter and softer than the southern breeze;
Strong as the hills, majestic as the seas;
Lovelier than all the tints upon the sky;
Higher than archangelic thrones on high;
Virgin most wonderful, divinest, best!
Immaculate, immortal, ever-blest!—
So sang they on; the burden of the strain
Meanwhile returning o'er and o'er again

(The same that he had lately caught afar),
" Ave Purissima, Purissima !"

Thus as they chanted thro' the woodland green,
He listening from his solitude unseen,
Meanwhile the lovely band with lightsome tread
Across the open interval had sped,
And now behind a turning to the right
Its rear was just receding out of sight,
When, gazing fixedly, within him sprang
A rapid, keen, insufferable pang
Of strong regret, to think so rare a prize
Was vanishing for ever from his eyes;
Breeding in turn a vehement desire
To follow on and join the sacred choir.
Till suddenly, as leaps the startled hare
From the close shelter of her ferny lair,
Up from his place, impatient of delay,
He rose, he sprang, all powerless to stay;
And by a secret fascination drawn
Pursued their footsteps o'er the flowery lawn.

To whom as now he drew more slowly near,
Strangely perplex'd between delight and fear,
Observing last behind, a youth, whose glance
Was wistfully surveying him askance,

As seemingly within his secret breast
More conscious of his presence than the rest,
He caught his floral vestment's golden braid,
And thus his eager supplication made:
"Say, youth divine, if mortal foot may dare
The same enamell'd sward with you to share?
For, having chanced to see you pass along,
So rare the sight, so ravishing the song,
I could not choose, so strong they wrought on
          me,
But follow after such fair company."

Then he in turn: "O Stranger, mortal eye
May seldom scan our mystic pageantry;
Much less hath poor mortality a part
Within our ranks; then, mortal as thou art,
Unless some special gift of Heav'n be thine,
Away! away! nor tempt the wrath divine!"

"But I the King himself of Heav'n above,
Present in His true Sacrament of love,
Here bear, by happy chance, upon my breast,
I, Euthanase, Franciscan monk and priest;
Who all unworthiness although I be,
Yet may His worth immense entreat for me."

Thus as he urged, through all the lengthen'd
    throng
A holy tremor seem'd to thrill along,
And he who spoke before, his gracious head
Devoutly bending, thus in answer said :
" Hail, Minister of praise to God above !
Hail, Minister to man of grace and love !
Priest of the Lord, Ambassador divine !
Preacher and Prophet of th' eternal Trine !
No higher dignity can earth bestow ;
No lovelier office Heav'n itself can show :
And Hail to Him, who present comes with thee
Veil'd in his Sacramental Mystery,
Whom we unveil'd, by yet superior grace
Ever behold in glory face to face ;
Thrice welcome thou to join our festive train,
Thrice happy we thy presence to obtain."

Thereat, with looks of joy and grateful pride,
He drew him unreluctant to his side,
And onward with the minstrel throng they sped,
Down the green openings of the leafy glade.

CANTO II.

The Three Holy Children.

SILENT at first, with secret awe impress'd,
  Unwonted tumults heaving in his breast,
The Priest his way pursued; and time had gone
Ere to a calmer mind subsiding down:
"Tell me," he cries, "O comrade heavenly fair,
Tell me (if it be lawful to declare)
Whether yon group so glitteringly bright,
That glides along inorb'd in liquid light,
Rightly mine inly-musing heart has guess'd
To be the same Three Children ever-blest,
Who in their Faith's high-soul'd integrity
Spurning the Babylonian king's decree,
Refused the golden image to adore
Set up in Dura's plain in days of yore?
Wherefore to them the sevenfold-heated flame
Like a soft cooling dewy breeze became,
And they within its fiery concave stood,
As though the covert of an arching wood

Did o'er their heads its budding branches fling
Breathing sweet fragrance of immortal Spring:
Wherein the while, unconscious of the blaze,
They hymn'd their royal Canticle of praise,
Amidst them, lo! an unexpected guest
Stood forth the Son of God to sight confess'd,
As on the Mount with His Apostles three,
And they transfigured shone as now I see,
In beatific brightness all divine,
As Saints imparadised in glory shine.
Say, am I right? or is the bright display
Rather some airy masquerade of May,
Such as the vacant mind might weave at will,
Lull'd in the sunbeams of the morning still?"

    To whom the other: "Well thy heart has guess'd:
Yon three are they, the Martyrs ever-blest,
Who rather than bend down adoring knee
In homage of a vain idolatry,
Contemning death, the fiery furnace chose
For their destruction heap'd by Israel's foes;
But One, amidst them there, from Heav'n appear'd;
Him the Chaldean Tyrant saw and fear'd;
Him the flame worship'd at its raving height,
Licking with trembling tongue his hand of might:

They all the while, within their shrine of fire,
As choristers within some golden choir,
Singing aloud in their sweet Maker's praise,
Unscathed, untainted, by the sevenfold blaze!
Therefore, when dying in an after-day
The Holy Children went in peace their way,
To them in memory of that Hymn was given
To lead the happy minstrelsy of Heaven;
Where evermore in glowing strains they sing
The glory manifold of glory's King,
Save when descending by the crystal stair
Which Angels secretly have shown them there,
At times to earth they come, and wind along
O'er dell and dale, with music and with song,
(Mostly when Spring has trick'd the groves
            anew,
And Nature wears her purest, loveliest hue),
A glistening Pageantry in green and gold,
Singing the selfsame Hymn they sang of old,
To that high Majesty whose hidden power
Sustains the force of Nature hour by hour,
And through the seasons, as they come and go,
Evolves the changes in perpetual flow.
Such the mysterious tones at morning clear
Borne from the coppice on the woodman's ear

And such the fleeting forms that interweave
Their golden glimpses with the mists of eve.
But if you ask me, whither this new dawn
So fast we speed along the dewy lawn,
Know that to Tintern's Sanctuary fair
We, early thus, on pilgrimage repair;
For thither, on this St. Augustin's Day,
Comes the great Lady of the Month of May,
With all her Court; and in her ancient pile
Hold festival the Saints of Britain's Isle,
In her Immaculate Conception's praise,
The late-defined Belief of earlier days."

  " Dear youth, thy news, exceeding all I sought,
Has fill'd me with amaze too deep for thought,"
The Priest replies ; " and hardly may I dare
Petition thee more fully to declare
Matters in such high mystery enshrined,
Unsuitable to this poor mortal mind."

  He in return, a smile of winning grace
Borne from the heart and beaming on his face ;
" To him whose ministry so high ascends
That at his feet all human grandeur bends,
Priest, Judge, and Deputy, of God most High,
What favour can our littleness deny ?

Know, therefore, since that day of evil doom
Which blotted out this realm from Christendom,
And cast the Faith of centuries away,
To unbelief and heresy a prey ;
Mary, still mindful of the seagirt Isle
That once so loved to bask beneath her smile,
And worshipp'd her as its especial Queen,
Like some fair lady in her own demesne,
Incessantly for England pour'd her sighs
From her empyreal faldstool in the skies,
To that dear Son of hers who reigns above,
Lord of illimitable grace and love,
And from th' eternal centre sweetly bends
The circling times to their appointed ends.
Nor pleaded She in vain, whose heart accords
In each desire so wholly with her Lord's ;
Whose lips perennial benedictions shower,
Omnipotent in prayer as He in power.

   " Long were the History, nor needs to tell
What thou already knowest but too well ;
How persecution all its vials pour'd
Upon the sacred remnant of the Lord
In this poor Isle,—yet still to Peter true,
In number as in strength the Faithful grew

Beneath Egyptian bondage; till at last,
Despite of Satan's pestilential blast,
Despite of bigotry's unhallow'd rage,
And all the frenzy of a godless age,
Once more establish'd by the Holy See
In sacred Hierarchic majesty
(Through him whose heart in Mary's is enshrined,
Immortal Pius, glory of mankind),
The Church of ancient days again uprose
In order bright confronting all its foes,
With serried ranks and every flag unfurl'd,
Boldly confess'd before a trembling world.

"Now therefore, when, for grievous trials past,
A second day of promise dawns at last,
And o'er the Isle of our dear Lady's love
In gifts of grace descends the heavenly Dove,
Encouraging so many, far and wide,
To glory in the Faith they once denied;
Fresh from the triumphs offer'd to her Name
By all the Christian realms with one acclaim
Upon occasion of th' august Decree
Of her Conception's peerless purity,
She makes a solemn progress through the land,
Duly escorted, with her virgin band,

Dispensing all around her, as she goes,
Gifts on her friends, and graces on her foes.
And meeting, oft and oft, along her way,
The sad memorials of a former day;
Morn after morn, she chooses from the rest
Some one or other which she loved the best,
Chantry or Abbey-Minster, once her own,
But now with waving eglantine o'ergrown;
And there, upon the sward of emerald green,
Holding her visitation as a Queen,
Where the High Altar stood in days gone by,
The heav'n's blue arch her only canopy,
Receives from Michael the Archangel's hand,
Guardian of sacred fabrics through the land,
Report exact of every crumbling wall,
Of each fair pillar nodding to its fall;
Of shatter'd arch and desecrated choir,
Altars defaced, and carvings burnt with fire;
Of chalices polluted, fonts defiled;
Of Rood and holy images despoil'd;
Of sacred vestments left to moth and rust;
Of glorious relics trampled in the dust;
Of virgins driven forth without a home;
Of monks condemn'd in banishment to roam;

Of all the long-neglected faithful dead;
Of all the tears by her sweet children shed;
O'er that same ruin'd pile without relief
For three long bitter centuries of grief!
Meanwhile around in solemn state appear
The Patron Saints of all the churches near,
And on their knees along the sacred sward,
Their Lady at their head, with one accord
In reparation pray of ancient crime,
And for a blessing on the coming time.

"Southwards from Holy Isle her course has
        wound
From step to step o'er consecrated ground :
By Hexham's fane; by Whitby's stormy steep,
Whence Hilda watches o'er the German deep;
By York's hoar minster; by the Ouse's bed,
Where Selby's Abbey lifts its mitred head;
By Beverley and Grantham, loved of yore;
By Croyland's ivied wreck, and many more;
A devious route—and now the golden morn
Which saw Augustin into glory born,
Augustin, your Apostle ever-blest,
Beholds her, on the borders of the West

(As on to Glastonbury with array
Of saintly retinue she holds her way),
Turning aside to Tintern's hallow'd walls,
Where peals the thrush its daily madrigals,
But dedicated once to God's high fame,
Beneath the shelter of the Virgin's name.
There, as we learn, 'tis purposed on this day,
Ere closes in the mystic Month of May,
On part of Britain, as the solemn meed
Of that high eminence so late decreed,
To place upon her brow the Crown of gold
In her Conception's praise prepared of old.
And for the sacred pomp, from far and near
The Sons of new Jerusalem repair.
We too were on our way, when in the shade
Of this green labyrinth our steps we stay'd,
To find the spot where once her Chapel stood
Down in the bosky hollow of the Wood,
And leave behind in largesses of grace
A vernal benediction on the place.
There in the Springs succeeding shall appear
The first new primrose of the opening year;
There shall the wren that owns the golden crest
Weave daintily at will her pensile nest:

No toad or adder make its slimy cell ;
No fever haunt, or noxious ague dwell.
Our task perform'd, to Tintern now with speed
Down the smooth sloping Severn we proceed,
Cistercian Tintern, pride of England's prime,
The journey long, but needing little time.
Thou too with us, if so thy heart impel,
Art free to go; but, oh ! bethink thee well,
This warning, Euthanase, to thee I give,
Hardly canst thou behold these things and live !"

    " And what to me," replies the godly man,
" A little shortening of this earthly span,
Compar'd with sight of Her, my blissful Queen,
Whom all this month I have entreating been,
That of her loving bounty she would send
To me, in Heav'n's best time, a happy end.
Oh, then, lead on ; for so but her I view,
Welcome to me whatever fate ensue."

    Thus as the two upon their way conversed,
Wholly in thoughts celestial immersed,
Meanwhile from haunt to haunt of coppice green,
O'er many a sunny glade that bask'd between,

Their course had sped; and now a twilight gray
Had o'er them closed, excluding half the day,
From the dense aromatic foliage shed
Of sombre pine-trees arching overhead,
Which on the tangled outskirts of the Wood
As sentinels in hoary grandeur stood.
Thence soon emerging on a terrace high,
They greet again the cheerful open sky,
And gazing forth upon the horizon wide,
Behold Salopia's Vale in all its pride,
A varied landscape, stretching far away,
Suffused with mist, or clear in morning's ray:
While at their feet Sabrina's waters gleam,
New swollen by romantic Morda's stream.

Thither obliquely slanting down the steep,
A path close-shaven by the nibbling sheep
Supplies them, in a straight continuous line,
A broad descent of scarce-perceived incline,
Whereby the margin gain'd, by rush and reed,
Through beds of nodding daffodil they thread,
Till, winding with the river's winding maze,
A sight of sudden beauty meets their gaze.
For close to where St. Oswy's ancient well
Up-bubbles from its arch'd and mossy cell,

Moor'd by a silver chainlet to the sward,
And as for some High Festival prepared,
In the smooth shelter of a mimic bay
A royal barge of state before them lay.
Antique in form as on the illumined page
Of some fair missal of the middle age,
Its curving prow, more graceful than the swan,
With scales of red and gold alternate shone;
Its hull with sparkling amethysts inlaid,
Figures of flying Cherubim display'd;
A woof of azure strew'd its spacious floor,
With lilies snowy-white enamell'd o'er;
While all of pearly plume its awning soft
On wands of twisted silver rose aloft,
With pennons hung, that ever as they play'd,
A lustre of prismatic rainbows made:
The whole, in its intensity of glow,
So deftly mirror'd in the flood below,
That of the duplicates 'twere hard to say
Which was the true, and which the phantasy.

As noted thus the Monk with rapid view,
The Pageant had embark'd; and ere he knew,
He found himself, some distance from the rest,
Sitting beneath the poop's o'erarching crest,

Whence droop'd majestically, fold in fold,
Mary's blue ensign with its cross of gold.
A moment more, and silently they sweep
Down the smooth current of the gliding deep.

———

CANTO III.

Sabrina.

O NATURE, type of Loveliness unseen!
Of Heav'n the mirror, and its mystic screen!
Ever to Euthanase his Lord and thine
Had giv'n to taste in thee a joy divine;
But never did the loveliest of thy sights
Entrance him with the rapture of delights
He felt as Severn's ancient windings down
In pomp majestical they glide along;
By perfum'd meads, by waving woodlands green,
Low shelvy banks of willow'd marge between;
Now in the broad'ning channel's mid career
Over a smooth expanse of waters clear;
Anon upon the river's shoaling edge,
Amidst a spiry growth of reeds and sedge;
By islets now with cowslip-plats impaved,
And now by knolls where silver aspens waved;
While ever, on each side, the landscape bright
Transfigured shone in more than earthly light,

Through intervolving wreaths of golden haze,
That in a halo of encircling rays
Attended them, disporting overhead,
As faster than the stream they onward sped,
Borne by a force innate; for oar was none,
Nor undulating sail, to urge them on,
Save only at the quiet helm there stood
He who had been the spokesman in the Wood,
And with a dainty finger's lightest play
Guided the bark upon her arrowy way.

Now ancient Shrewsbury appears in sight,
Rising on her peninsulated height;
Fair-abbey'd formerly, ere Faith's decline,
Guardian of Wenifrida's golden shrine.
Invisible to all, unguess'd, unheard
(As in each listless countenance appear'd),
Beneath the stately bridges smooth they glide,
And circle round the city's terrac'd side,
In noble sweep; by many a villa fair,
By castellated height and mossy stair;
By lime-tree avenues, and gardens gay,
And painted pleasure-boats that idle lay,
And open casements trellis'd o'er with flowers,
And bastions worn and coronals of towers;

High above all a pillar'd heavenly glow
Distinguishing meanwhile the site below,
Where Holy Church, unwearied to the last,
Uprears amid the ruins of the past,
With patient hope, and love that conquers death,
The Sanctuary new of ancient Faith!
Well pleased our Euthanase the token views;
But quickly melts the scene in distant hues,
As, coursing on by wold and slanting wood,
They thread the long meanders of the flood.

Anon in front the Wrekin towering high
Stamps its projecting outline on the sky;
And, on a smooth incline of margin green,
Fair Bildas Abbey to the right is seen,
By woodlands back'd, by hanging woodlands
            crown'd,
A precious relic set with emeralds round!

There by the thymy bank their course they stay'd,
Beneath an old wych-elm's o'erspreading shade,
Then disembarking up the sward ascend,
And round the massive pillars slowly wend
In solemn state, with censers waving high,
And Mary's immemorial litany,

And chanted requiem that plaintive rose
For all the Brotherhood who there repose:
Which o'er, again their bark the current cleaves,
While thus his laden heart the Monk relieves;
" Adieu, sweet Abbey of the tuneful dead !
Fair vision of a time for ever fled !
Long as the Severn rolls her silver tide,
May she behold thee seated at her side.
Oh, happier far in naked ruin laid !
Thy name forgotten, and thy stones decay'd !
Than in primeval splendour standing left
But of interior majesty bereft,
To shine in gilded chains the spoiler's prey,
And home of every doctrine of the day;
Adorn'd without, a sepulchre within,
The patient tool of heresy and sin !"

Meanwhile the banks, as on they gaily glide,
With gradual slope ascend on either side,
Till breaking into rocks of dusky red,
They form a thickly-foliaged cleft o'erhead,
Where ash and birch display their leaflets new
In contrast with the holly's darker hue,
And lines of copse unbrokenly descend
Down to the brink, and with the current blend.

Long flats succeed of water-meadows green,
With rills that dance along in sparkling
     sheen;
Young larch plantations, timber cut and piled,
Cornfields in early blade, and moorlands wild.
Then in a lake-like and majestic reach,
High-terraced and o'erhung with hoary beech,
The river broadly marching bears them on
Beneath the heights of Bridgenorth's airy town;
And on again, in many a graceful twine,
By Bewdley's olden Sanctuary-shrine;
By lordly seats embosom'd deep in trees,
Abodes of ancient state or modern ease;
By spacious parks, where groups of deer arc
     seen
Browsing at leisure in the glades serene;
By downs of gorse that all the air perfume,
By hamlets rude, and orchards pink with bloom,
To Worcester's hoary fane: anon in sight
Malvern's gray abbey rises on the right;
And now a tidal stream, through pastures
     brave,
Sabrina bears them on a tawnier wave,
Buried at times betwixt embankments steep,
Down to her outlet on th' Atlantic deep.

O Memory, dear Paintress of the past!
How long, how vividly, thy pictures last!
Or, if they fade, how quickly they revive
With all the warmth of life again alive!
True as the ray-impencill'd solar print!
Brighter than Claude's or Titian's glowing tint!
So found our Euthanase, as on they speed
By Tewkesbury, across the purple mead,
Through whose deep bosom, singing as she goes,
Poetic Avon down from Evesham flows.
For where the sister rivers blend their tide,
Like two fair doves descending side by side,
Pursuing with his glance a sunny gleam
Up the slant opening of the younger stream,
A distant landscape on his vision fell,
Which, piercing recollection's inmost cell,
All in a trice dissolved his heart in tears,
Smit with a cruel grief of former years.
Whereat the youthful helmsman at his side
The change detecting which he strove to hide,
His hand with tender feeling took and press'd,
As conscious of the trouble at his breast,
Essaying to unlock its hidden source
With honeyed words of soft persuading force.

"Oh, say, dear friend, what secret cloud is
　　　this,
Thus raining tear-drops in a time of bliss?
A portion of thy grief on me bestow;
Imparted anguish loses half its woe.
Oft unexpected comes long-sought relief,
And I may comfort have to soothe thy grief."

Then he: "Alas! what power in nature dwells
To stir the depth of sorrow's hidden cells!
For as but now by Avon's stream we pass'd,
I chancing up its course a glance to cast,
In the far blue the Bredon hills espied,
Dear Mounts of God! upon whose further side,
Basking serene in happy vernal skies,
My native vale, the Vale of Evesham, lies;
(Evesham, of early Faith the sacred fold,
For Mary's Apparition famed of old;)
A moment's glimpse,—and yet it served to bring
The Tragedy of my first boyhood's spring,
Across the disc of thought with such a pain,
As it were all enacting o'er again.

" Beneath an early-widow'd mother's eye
'Twas there my life's young morning glided by,

Myself her only child, but not alone;
Another charge she had beside her own :
A boy and girl, twin orphans passing fair,
Left by a dying school-mate to her care.
Our age the same, with them my childhood
      grew,
Apart from theirs no joy or sorrow knew,
With them together learnt, together play'd,—
A sunny track of time without a shade.
But what entwined us more than all the rest
Each in the other's young and ardent breast,
Was that dear flower of love our Mother nursed
So patiently within us from the first,
For Him who on the Cross of Calvary died,
And Her who stood in anguish at His side—
Jesus and Mary.   Ah, how would the tears
Their cups o'erbrim, while in our eager ears
Oft and again she plaintively would tell
The tender story of that sad farewell,
Woven in such variety of ways
As never have I heard in after days!
Ah, what delight, from that devotion born,
Was ours, on each recurring festal morn,
Our Chapel Altar duly to prepare
With all that we could find of rich and rare,

And deck our Lady's image like a bower
With many a fragrant and exotic flower,
Then at the Mass in blended parts to sing
Sweeter than all the songsters of the Spring!
One thought meanwhile upon our hearts impress'd,
And in the fairest hues of fancy dress'd,
Grew with our growth, and gain'd, I know not how,
A secret force at which I marvel now,
England's Conversion!—Oh! with what desire
Did this high cause our little bosoms fire!
For this, how fervently to Heaven we pray'd!
For this, how many plans of life we laid!
For this, how oft beneath the summer boughs,
Lady of Evesham, pour'd to Thee our vows!

" But time sped on; and we might number now
As many happy Springs perchance as thou,
When, as it fell, my Theodore and I,
On this same Feast, some sixty years gone by,
Having, at our exulting mother's side,
Our First Communion made at morningtide,
Went out at noon, in very height of bliss,
Each cheek imprinted with a tender kiss,
Into the blooming meadow-lands to play
With other boys, companions for the day.

Where so it was, a lad, in idle sport,
A sudden rivalry betwixt us wrought,
Saying that Theodore (a tale untrue)
Boasted himself best swimmer of the two
Behind my back.—Alas! from little things
How large a growth of evil often springs!
For, seated as we were on Avon's marge,
I, miserable, heedless of the charge
So oft enjoin'd us by maternal fear,
Never to bathe without attendance near,
Stung with ambition, pointed in my pride
To a white lily twinkling in the tide,
And challenged Theodore the stream to breast
And for the flowery prize with me contest.
Which he accepting, overcome at last
By boyish taunts against his courage cast,
We strip, and straight upon the sign agreed
Skim through the glassy flood with all our
          speed,
Amidst huzzas;—he leading first, till I
With a strong eager effort pass him by,
And in my clasp triumphantly enfold
The snow-white chalice with its beads of gold.
Which to the turfy bank I scarce had brought,
When, lo! a cry that Theodore was caught

And struggling with the weeds.—Ah, what a dart
Of anguish on the instant smote my heart!
I speeded back.—Nowhere could he be seen;
Anon he rose close by, with smile serene,
Unutterable, greeting my fond gaze;
Then down again beneath the watery maze
Was lost!—I dived into the fatal spot,
Again, and yet again,—but found him not,
Till the fourth time.   Then all too weak to rise
Down at his side I lay, and death mine eyes
Had with his icy touch for ever seal'd,
But that some mowers from a neighbouring field
Came up, and drew us from the limpid deep,
As on its pebbly bed we lay asleep,
Both corpses in appearance, face to face,
Lock'd in a last and brotherly embrace.

" The rest I pass—my own recovery slow;
My mother's piteous uncomplaining woe;
The tears of Rosalie conceal'd in vain,
From tenderest fear of adding to my pain;
Bright Theodore in silent darkness laid
With solemn dirge beneath the cypress shade,
Bearing in folded beauty on his breast
My lily at so dear a cost possess'd.

But what consumed me more than all beside
Was the keen consciousness that he had died
In disobedience, and that through me—
Daily this thought renew'd its poignancy;
Nor could our Priest with all his gentle art
Extract its barb of anguish from my heart.
For Theodore, for Theodore e'en still   .
Th' unbidden pang will oft my bosom thrill;
For him, so many years among the dead,
This very morn my tearful Mass was said."

He ceased; and thus, with looks of pleasant
          cheer,
The youthful helmsman softly in his ear:
" O Euthanase, thy brother weep no more;
Long since he gain'd in peace the heavenly
          shore,
There in perpetual joyance to abide
With his beloved ones seated at his side;
All save thyself here dragging on thy years,
A lonely pilgrim in a vale of tears,
Lost to him long, yet e'en on Sion's hill
Amidst eternal sweets remember'd still.
Nay, what if love of thee have drawn him nigh,
And Theodore himself be standing by !"

Thus as he spoke, across the other's soul
A mystic feeling gradually stole,
Such as the dying have when on their eyes
Closes this world with all its vanities;
Nor yet, except a trembling fringe of dawn,
The curtains of the next are open drawn.
With earnest look the speaker he surveys,
Doubts his own judgment, doubts his very
       gaze;
For underneath the helmsman's form conceal'd,
The comrade of his youth now stood reveal'd!
Taller and older somewhat than of yore
He seem'd; and nestling in his bosom bore
A snow-white Lily whence all Eden breathed,
The smile of other days his lips enwreathed;
Clear shone his eye, and on his damask cheek
Sate rosy health. Thrice Euthanase to speak
Essay'd, and thrice his tongue refused a word,
Until, by tender glances re-assured,
It came at last. "And is it thou indeed,
My Theodore! from death's Elysian mead
Hither return'd, whom these dim eyes behold;
Beloved companion of the days of old?
Oh, joy of joys! Wrapt in the tomb's embrace,
Little I thought again to see thy face,

Save where on memory's tablet it appears
Gleaming for ever through a mist of tears!
Oh, say, dear brother-chorister of mine!
By that true bond of melody divine
Which link'd us as two birds on one same spray,
Singing together to the leaves of May.—
Sweet yoke-fellow in heavenly harmonies!—
Oh, say, since thou hast pass'd into the skies,
Hast thou forgiven me that guilty day
When all too far I tempted thee to stray,
Borne upon Avon's gently flowing wave
To thy sad lily-mantled early grave?
Oh, how with thee, cut off in boyhood's bloom,
Went down my heart of hearts into the tomb!
What cruel self-reproach my bosom tore!
How long the penance! the remorse how sore!"

" Ah, deem not, Brother best," the youth replied,
" Deem not thy Theodore too early died.
Early and late are all alike to those
Who go with their dear Saviour to repose.
To me, from infancy, the Lord of grace
Imparted a desire to seek His face;
And oft in boyhood's hour, when none were by,
I made my prayer that I might early die,

To the sweet Mother of the King of kings,
Smit with the beauty of eternal things.
That prayer was heard.　By vanity betray'd,
I broke the law maternal love had made.
Guilty the deed; yet not in guilt I died;
One contrite act of love for all supplied;
And, ere I knew, I found myself received,
Oh, mercy greater than I had believed!
In that blue vestibule which nearest lies
To the clear golden gates of Paradise.
Not Heaven: for still some penalty was due
To God the infinitely just and true;
Not Heaven: for thither, at a later day,
'Twas thy first Mass that open'd me the way;
Not Heaven: but a most heavenly calm retreat,
Patient abode of expectation sweet;
Where no regret consumes, no fear o'erwhelms,
Mildest of all the Purgatorial realms.
There, Euthanase, oh, how for thee I sigh'd,
Imperill'd still upon the treacherous tide!
Oh, how for thee I pray'd through many a
　　　year
While dark and dubious did thy fate appear,
Securer now.—But, as I think, 'tis time
Thou wert prepared for that emprise sublime

Which thou hast enter'd on. Now, therefore, take
This Lily for thy Theodore's dear sake,
And oft as thy too feeble human gaze
Shall quail before the pure empyreal blaze
About to dawn on thee in all its power,
The scent ambrosial of this fair flower
Thy spirit shall exalt, high things to see
Exceeding far all natural imagery."

Therewith the pearly chalice trick'd with gold,
Sad object of their rivalry of old,
But now bedropp'd with Paradisal dew,
And sacred earnest of a friendship new,
Committing to his hands, he closely press'd
The old Franciscan to his youthful breast,
From whence a warmth so rich, so glowing came,
Diffused transportingly through all his frame,
That in his heart, by freezing years subdued,
Youth, boyhood, infancy, seem'd all renew'd;
And, spite of age's locks of wint'ry gray,
He feels once more a very child of May!

Meanwhile they fast had cleaved the yellow
    deep;
And opening now into a broader sweep,

No more between impending banks controll'd,
Severn a noble estuary roll'd,
When, slowly issuing from the osier'd shore
Where stood St. Arvan's hermitage of yore,
A fleet majestical appear'd in view
Of stately swans in plumes of snowy hue,
Which, parting presently on either side,
Drew up around them in a circle wide;
Ring within ring, in orderly array,
As though to be their escort on the way.
Amidst whose movements, lo! with sudden
　　　　burst,
Again the Chant had risen as at first,
The chant of May, glad Nature's jubilee,
With peal on peal of " Benedicite,"
Inviting all around, below, above,
Lovely creations of the God of love:
Islets, and waving woods, and pastures green,
Moving along in panoramic scene;
The fallow uplands shelving from the hills;
The meadows fattening on the tinkling rills;
The grazing herds that dot the distant shore;
The porpoise slowly heaving o'er and o'er;
The birds that glance athwart, or idly rest,
Rocking to sleep upon the billow's breast;

The fleecy clouds, the sunlight, and the breeze,
Earth, sky, and sea, with all their harmonies;
Superlatively Him to bless and praise
Who moves the mystic wheels of Nature's maze,
Thro' height, thro' depth, wherever worlds extend,
Sweetly disposing all things to their end,
In Unity and Trinity confess'd
Immutable, eternal, ever-blest!
Then in a swell melodious borne aloft,
" Ave Purissima," in cadence soft,
Amidst the forest of sweet tones upsprang
Like some aerial palm; the while they sang
Of Her, creation's paragon and pride,
Surpassing all created things beside:
Mary, the joy of the most joyant Trine!
Mary, of grace the coronal divine!
Mary, of nature the quintessence bright!
The earth's high miracle, the Heav'n's delight!
Whom earth and Heav'n Immaculate proclaim,
Mother of Him from whom all nature came,
Mother of men and Virgin bliss of May,
To whom all natural things their homage pay!

Then in mellifluous harmony combined,
Like threads of gold and silver intertwined,

Subtly the chants inwove themselves in one,
Each lost in each, yet losing not its own ;
So deftly interlacing, it were vain
To trace the curious joinings of the strain.
And ever as they sang, the minstrels threw
Fair flowers around, in wreaths of every hue,
Upon the tawny flood, which, as they fell,
Itself refining by a secret spell,
Clear and pellucid grew as living light,
Or element of liquid crystal bright !
And ever still, as on the galley swept,
The swans their snowy ring unbroken kept,
Till rounding sharp a headland, lo ! its sea
The Bristol Channel opens broad and free,
Gleaming with sails.   Anon upon the right,
Guarding the Wye's low outlet, comes in sight
St. Tecla's hallow'd Isle, where wont of yore
Pilgrims to meet for Palestina's shore.

Thither they shot abrupt : and, as they near'd,
It seem'd a thousand angel faces peer'd
Forth from a glory that around it hung ;
It seem'd a thousand Alleluias rung ;
Then glancing by, up Vaga's stream they sped,
To where monastic Chepstow lifts her head,

Slid arrowlike beneath th' embattled keep
Where Monmouthshire's old feudal glories sleep;
And on—through winding depths of sylvan shade,
By many a rocky height and sloping glade,
By pinnacles that from the water rise
Fantastical as Nature can devise,
By semicircling bends of margin green,
By smooth enamell'd meads that lie between,
By crags which immemorial woods sustain,
By hanging woods o'ertopp'd with crags again,
To Tintern's ancient Sanctuary glide
On the clear bosom of th' ascending tide.

CANTO IV.

Tintern.

O THOU dear relic of a happier day!
　Fair in thy bloom, still fair in thy decay!
Amidst thy foliaged hills embosom'd round
In silent depths of solitude profound,
Far from the tumults of a world unblest,
A lovely vision of celestial rest!
Tintern! how many blithesome Mays had pass'd
Since thou and Euthanase had parted last!
Yet e'en upon his childhood's tender mind
So firm an impress hadst thou left behind,
That, as again his wistful eyes survey'd
Thy rising form emboss'd in sun and shade,
At once, like some medallion of gold
Fitted again into its ancient mould,
His memory's inward image, line for line
And touch for touch, resolved itself in thine!
Another reach, and on the buoyant tide
Beneath the Abbey precincts calm they glide.

E

There, to the sloping marge as they drew nigh,
Lo! on its breadth of green declivity,
A band of Harpers seated row in row,
With long descending beards as white as snow,
Their brows antique with budding oak-leaf bound,
Their necks with silver rings encircled round,
From whose accordant strokes in dulcet swell
Bursts of harmonious welcome rose and fell;
A bardic throng; with one who seem'd their
       head,
And on a golden lyre the Pæan led.
In purple robe and panoply of state
On a triumphal car aloft he sate,
Drawn by two antler'd stags, who meekly stand
In trappings bright, obedient to command.
Of whom thus Theodore, interpreting
The other's glance: " Behold the Cambrian King!
Teudric, who cast his regal crown aside,
And here a hermit lived, a martyr died,
(Borne by two stags, so holy legends say,
Wounded and fainting from the Pagan fray),
Long ere the Abbey with its tuneful bells
Awoke the echoes of the woodland dells.
Now o'er the Solitude he loved of yore
He reigns its Guardian Saint for evermore!

Hail, Martyr King!" Thus as he spoke, the barge
Its numbers had outpour'd upon the marge,
And marshall'd from his chariot, two and two,
By that high Seneschal in order due,
Skirting a ruin'd length of cloister gray,
The sacred pomp proceeded on its way.

   Silent and slow, behind the minstrel choir,
His heart with expectation all on fire,
Follow'd the monk his Theodore beside;
When on the left a wicket open wide
Discloses, through a moss-grown arch, to sight,
An orchard in a blooming flush of white;
There they turn in; the rest their course pursue,
And round the winding way are lost to view.
" To meet our sacred Lady they proceed,"
Said Theodore; " but thou, most dear, take heed,
And if within thy breast there linger yet
One earthborn hope, affection, or regret,
Purge it at once, for all is heavenly here,
Nor may with worldly dross admixture bear.
Breathe but a single wish, a single sigh,
For aught of mutabilities gone by,
And all thou seest—rapt from thee away—
Dissolves for ever like a dream of day !"

" Fear not lest such an evil me betide,"
The son of sainted Francis quick replied ;
" For if, so far in years, myself I know,
Neither in Heav'n above nor earth below
Is aught that I desire, except it be
The Vision of my sweetest God to see,
And of that Lady in her splendour bright
Whom thy report has promised to my sight."

A smile of tenderest pity, as of one
To whom in God the hidden things are known,
And all the frailties to our state allied,
Rippled his cheek.   " Ah, Euthanase," he sigh'd,
" Little the soul of her true weakness knows,
Till off this cheating mortal coil she throws ;
And oft she finds, by sad experience taught,
The world far stronger in her than she thought.
Still in the heart, with difficulty wean'd,
Some earthly phantom lingers to the end ;
E'en still, though mortified to present things,
To some affection of the past it clings ;
Revivifies delights for ever fled,
And loves as living whom it mourns as dead !"

He paused ; but Euthanase his spirit check'd,
Conscious within of manifold defect,

And breathing forth a sigh to Him who sees
Each heart with all its hidden miseries,
Beneath o'er-roofing blossoms held his way,
Till forth he steps into the open day,
Where in a mead which peaceful heifers graze
The Abbey Church its Eastern end displays.

All beautiful it stood, so fresh and fair,
'Twas difficult to feel that death was there,
A sadly soothing scene!   Whereon the while
He gazed with tears he could not all beguile,
As on the bier of some fair vestal maid
In saintly sleep before the altar laid:
" O Theodore, rememberest thou," he cried,
" How once before, at our dear mother's side,
Here we stood gazing, when in childhood's day,
On such another pleasant morn of May,
Hither she brought us with thy sister fair
To show us what the former glories were?
And how upon the sod she made us kneel
And say an Ave for our country's weal,
That once again poor England might enjoy
The Faith which she had gloried to destroy?
And now how many years are past and gone,
Yet still in heresy she lingers on!

Still spurns the hand outstretch'd to heal her
        woes !
Still on her course of ruin blindly goes,
From bad to worse, from worse to worse again,
As though for her return all prayer were vain !"

" Who change the truth of God into a lie,
Tough is the knot their children must untie,"
His friend in turn. " Yet, O my Brother, know
Things are not wholly as they seem below,
And through this Island such a work of grace
Already has begun and moves apace,
That at th' unwonted mercy in amaze
The very Angels tremble as they gaze.
But, hark ! what chanted anthem, soft and clear,
Forth floating from the choir salutes mine ear ?"

Thus as he spoke, upon the balmy air
Uprose distinctly, as from monks at prayer,
A solemn, plaintive, melancholy strain,
That brought the Lamentations back again
Of Holy Week : " How lone in its decay
Lies the fair glory of a former day !
How mourneth Holy Church her ancient home,
So ruin'd all and desolate become !

O quit the path thy guilty feet have trod,
Return, return thee, England, to thy God!

"The ways of Sion mourn; her sighs ascend
Because so few her solemn Feasts attend,
Her gates are broken down, her altars rent;
Her priests and virgins in her aisles lament.
O England, see the ruin thou hast made;
Return, return thee, whence thy feet have stray'd!

"Weeping, fair Sion's Daughter weeps to see
Oppressors ruling in her Sanctuary;
A nation once her own her name despise,
And all her lovers turn'd to enemies.
O England, quit the path which thou hast trod,
Return, return thee to thy Lord and God!"

A dying close—and all was still again;
But Euthanase, held captive by the strain,
Was standing rapt, when Theodore his mind
Recalling with a touch, an arm entwined
In his; and him, as one in vision, led
Across the fragrant cowslip-mantled mead,
To where, all basking in a summer glow,
The Southern Transept show'd its portal low.

"Our entrance see," he cries; "but thou, dear
        friend,
To what I do with earnest heed attend,
And do the same." Therewith across his breast
Salvation's Sign he drew, and forward press'd
The yielding door;—a moment, and a prayer,
Pausing, he breathes upon the trembling air,
The next—and round them hush'd in calm re-
        pose
Thy lovely walls, Cistercian Tintern, rose!

   Silent they gazed. Serene and bright it lay
The same as when beheld in childhood's day,
A sylvan Temple! where for pavement fair
Of intersecting marbles rich and rare
The sward of centuries had spread a floor,
Smooth as the printless sand upon the shore;
Where for emblazon'd roof the open sky
Display'd its blue unclouded canopy;
Where over shafted pillar, hanging wall,
Mullion and groin and arch symmetrical,
Ivy of eld its glossy folds had wound,
And draped itself in rich festoons around;
While pennon-like from every crossing height
Saplings of ash and oak in golden light

Hung tremulous.   Nor wanted flow'rets there
For altars, had they been ; nor to the air
Wanted exuberance of incense sweet
Outbreathed from hidden beds of violet ;
So tenderly had wrought thy touch divine,
Nature, dear haunter of the ruin'd shrine!
Coming a gentle mourner, day by day
With patient love to beautify decay,
And using all the craft thy fingers can
To make atonement for the wreck of man !

Silent they gazed.   'Twas vacant all and still ;
No sound except the nestling's smother'd trill—
No footfall up or down—no form in sight—
The smile of day, the solitude of night !
Another glance—and as at morning-tide,
Adown the Nave of some Cathedral wide,
When the first beams of early twilight faint
Begin the storied windows to impaint,
Figures and draperies of varied hue
By unperceived degrees emerge to view ;
At first, a tinted maze without design,
Then radiating, forming, line by line,
Till cluster'd thick in many a noble band
Virgins and Martyrs forth in glory stand ;

So now—for where the sunbeams send apace
Through the tall Eastern window's empty space
Full on the grassy floor their flood of light,
Lo, figures dimly breaking on the sight!
Till, as from some interior depth conceal'd,
A living group of monks itself reveal'd!

Clear in the floodgate of the orient tide,
The Chancel down, some twenty of a side,
Upon the sward they knelt, in act of prayer,
Distinct in tunic, cowl, and scapular,
Cistercians all—their eyelids downward bent,
Their lips compress'd in silence eloquent,
Their arms devoutly cross'd.—Anon they rise,
And through the ruin'd Nave procession-wise
With miserere chant, and cleansing spray
Of lustral waters scatter'd on their way,
Their Abbot last of all, in solemn state
Go slowly wending to the Western gate,
There issue forth, and ranged on either hand,
Outside the Abbey-Minster take their stand.
Whom following observant close behind
The twain among the rest a station find.

CANTO V.

Tu Purissima.

O THOU dear gentle glory of the skies!
  Fair Mother-Maid and Queen of Paradise!
Who ever wert so bountiful to me,
And art so high in grace and dignity
That to conceive Thee as Thou art indeed
Doth all our human intellect exceed!
Thus far an easy course my bark has steer'd ;—
But now, the risk approaching which I fear'd
E'en from the first, I tremble with dismay
Lest I should aught of Thee unworthy say.
Ah then, I ask, dear Poetess divine,
By that melodious Canticle of thine
Whose words enchant the world, assist the need
Of him who writes, nor less of those who read,
That while of mystical realities
Dimly I sing beneath an earthly guise,
They of my parable may judge aright,
Nor of diviner sense oblivious quite

Haply a lower meaning take away,
Where I had aim'd a higher to convey.

Now gazing from the Western front around,
In silence of expectancy profound,
Upon the foliaged hills that facing rise,
Our Euthanase a lovely scene espies.
For where upon the left the rocks are piled
From ledge to ledge in woody medley wild,
Parting the copse a breadth of greenest glade
In ample and majestic sweep display'd
Gradual ascends, until its topmost height
Far up among the hills is lost to sight.
Along its either side, from end to end,
Tall May-trees in the pride of bloom extend,
Alternate pink and white, and form a screen
From blustering winds; within whose space serene
The busy sun-motes swarm upon the air,
As by instinctive force attracted there;
While all the smooth incline of verdant floor,
With buttercups besprinkled richly o'er,
Shows like a tapestry of gold and green
Laid for the solemn entry of a Queen!

Whereon the while his yearning vision fed
As on some avenue that Heavenward led,

A stair for visitant Archangels made,
An emerald stair with topazes inlaid,—
Along the slanting woods a flourish shrill
Of clarions rang, and from behind the hill,
Down the fair alley'd breadth of golden glade
Gaily advanced a glistening cavalcade.

Knights of St. John they seem'd, as might be
        guess'd
From the white Cross of Malta on their breast;
As three and three, in burnish'd armour bright,
With open casques that gave the face to sight,
With nodding plumes and swords that flash'd a
        flame,
Erect upon their prancing barbs they came,
The type authentical and pattern high
Of manhood, worth, and dauntless chivalry!
To pure virginity and honour vow'd,
Each in his mien a virgin honour show'd;
Each on his shield the badge of Mary bore;
Each on his lip a smile of triumph wore,
A smile sedate of triumph nobly gain'd,
Of triumph irreversibly obtain'd!
For now from Paynim wars return'd at last,
Their desperate Crusade for ever past,

They seem'd as those in saintly glory blest,
Who in their God of all in all possess'd,
No more of trials here and earthly pain
Can e'en the faint remembrance wake again!
Slowly they came amid the sunny gleam,
Soft as a breath and silent as a dream;
Then to the Abbey Church as near they drew
A blast upon their banner'd trumpets blew,
And wheeling right and left upon the green,
As guard of honour there await their Queen.

Whereat, as up the slope his glance again
The Monk directs, a venerable train
He sees with measured step advancing nigh,
Whose weeds of serge, whose scrip and rosary,
The bonnet gray betrick'd with scallop shells,
The girdle hung about with tinkling bells,
The naked feet, of penitence the sign,
The staff enwreathed with palm of Palestine,
Proclaim them to be Pilgrims from afar,
The Pilgrims of the Holy Sepulchre!
Ah me! what burdens in their time they bore
Of toil and stint and tribulation sore!
How rough, how perilous, had been the way!
How scant the rest, how weary the delay!

But now to Eden-land restored at last,
Their life-long pilgrimage for ever past,
Joy in their eye, and gladness in their song,
A vision of repose they came along;
And seem'd, all suffering forgotten quite
In the clear reflex of immortal light,
To find, oh, incommensurable gain!
A Heaven of bliss for every earthly pain.

Then over hill and woodland, vale and mead,
Began a new and fairer grace to spread;
More golden grew the light, more blue the sky,
On balmier wing the zephyr floated by;
And livelier still in leaf and budding spray
The secret pulse of nature seem'd to play,
As though some hidden elemental force
Were stirring at creation's inner source,
And with the beauty of their second birth
Clothing before their time the things of earth.
With thrilling heart he mark'd the change appear,
And knew that May's fair glory must be near!

"She comes, She comes!" cried Theodore,
　　and lo!
Along the height a glancing to and fro

Of splendours soft; whence like a lovely
       thought
Into its shape from teeming fancies wrought:
Or some rich efflorescence of the morn;
Or incense, of the breathing meadows born;
Virgins behind and virgins on each side,
Appear'd the Eternal Spirit's Virgin Bride!
A form of light, a form of beauty fair,
Seated serene, in floods of golden hair,
Upon a milk-white steed of heavenly mould,
Such as the Saint of Patmos saw of old
Bearing victoriously upon his way
The Conqueror of death in dread array,
Amidst exulting wafts of saintly song,
Majestically sweet She came along,
In dawning youth, for so it seem'd to be,
Unless 'twere rather youth's eternity!
Above her queenly head with step sedate
Virgins support a canopy of state
Fluttering with doves, that like a halo play
Circling and crossing in the sunny ray;
While in advance two Princes, side by side,
Each with a pearly wand, the Pageant guide,
Each in himself a marvel to the gaze,
So dazzling in immortal glory's blaze!

"Of Albion and of Rome th' Apostles high!"
Thus Theodore, "twin Saints in majesty!
Augustin, who dissolved our pagan night!
And Philip, sweetest of the Saints in light,
Our Isle's new guest! Their Festal-day the same,
An equal place by Mary's side they claim
This happy morn. Oh, see how, zone in zone,
Their friendly aureoles blend themselves in one!"

"O lovely Pair! thus ever hand in hand
Lead on our sacred Lady through the land!"
The Priest rejoins. "But, dearest heart, declare,
You troop of virgins so surpassing fair,
That comes behind—by what exalted name
In England's sacred Chronicle of fame,
Must I to their high presence worship pay?"
"St. Ursula and her Companions they,"
He answered, "leaders in the glorious line
Of virgin Saints that Providence divine
To Britain lent; whom follow, side by side,
St. Hilda, Abbess; and St. Winifride
The rose of Wales, with more of like degree;
And last our Holy Children of Chaldee:
Oh, how their former lustre paling seems
Before a newer glory's brighter beams!"

Meanwhile, from either side the Western
    Gate,
Advancing in processionary state
With glad Magnificat, and tapers bright,
And fragrant incense-wreaths of snowy white,
The Abbey Monks in reverent order drawn
Had occupied the centre of the lawn ;
And silent stood, their Abbot at their head
In amice, alb, and precious cope, array'd,
Bearing, irradiant in gems and gold,
A Crucifix most lovely to behold.
Whither, as nearer now our Lady drew,
All Paradise seem'd opening on the view. .
Oh, vision exquisite! Oh, form and face
The very mould and utterance of grace!
Oh, head seraphical! oh, dovelike eyes!
Oh, bloom incarnadined in Heaven's own dyes!
Oh, mien all-gracious, blending into one
Meekness and most august dominion!
As on in flowing azure folds she came,
Borne on a wave of jubilant acclaim,
In maiden majesty! Ideal blest
Of all that highest genius ever guess'd!
Of all that e'er on contemplation's eye
In visions dawn'd of saintliest ecstasy!

So the Franciscan felt; and in the view
Was conscious of a grace divinely new:
He saw, he gazed, and ravish'd in the sight
Seem'd at the life-spring of immortal light
To quaff exuberant joy.   Yet e'en with this
A vivid sense possess'd his heart's abyss,
That he of that magnificence so fair
But saw what his mortality could bear;
Its outer gloss alone to sight reveal'd,
The rest in its own majesty conceal'd!

Thus as She came with winning grace benign,
The Abbot our Redemption's loving sign
Upraised, and as mid-way upon the green
The Pageant stay'd, forthwith to our dear Queen
Presented it; which, after reverence due,
She kissing with a tenderness that drew
From Euthanase's eyes the startled tear,
Alighted soft as falling gossamer,
And through the traceried arch-way pass'd along
Into the Nave with all her virgin throng.

" O dear espousèd City of the skies !
My pilgrimage's hope and promised prize !

Are, then, my early fancies coming true,
And do I here indeed thy glories view ?"
Thus Euthanase, as entering now again
Unnoticed in the rear of Mary's train,
His eyes a wondering glance, O Tintern, throw
Upon thy heights above and aisles below.
For all was changed.—A scene of ruin still,
But ruin by a grace ineffable
Transfigured, glorified !—As when a child
Across a picture faded and defiled
Rays from a prism sends ; or, as the hand
Of poesy but waves its magic wand,
And common things are seen in beauty new ;
Or as upon a pearly shell we view
Tracings in gold ; or as the quarried stone
By vivid touches into outline grown
Gives forth, in perfect symmetry reveal'd,
The form of beauty it before conceal'd !
He felt the sacred spell, and silent stood
As one transfix'd. In such a glistening flood
The walls were bathed ; each stone a living
      gem,
As though from Heaven the New Jerusalem
Had come, and mid the haunts of ruin green
Her clear foundations set, a sparkling sheen

Of jasper, emerald, and topaz bright,
Of jacinth, beryl, sapphire, chrysolite,
Till all was made divine!　Nor wanted there
Such anthem as with Sion's City fair
Might well accord, from all the saintly throng
Rising in one full harmony of song:
" Hail, Mary, hail! conceived without a stain!
Come, Lady, come and in thy glory reign.
Virgin of God, receive the Crown of praise,
The Crown prepared thee from eternal days!"

So went the strain, as up the glittering aisle,
Gladness and benediction in her smile,
Our Lady pass'd amidst her maiden band
With those Apostles still on either hand,
To where, mid-way upon the velvet sward,
Fronting the choir, a faldstool stood prepared.
When, lo! the virgins who had charge beside
The Heaven's eternal and unsullied Bride,
Around her shoulders, as she knelt in prayer,
A mantle drew most excellently rare,
Ermine within, a mystic maze without
Of gold and divers colours interwrought;
With which no web of India might vie,
Nor finest leaf of Nature's 'broidery.

Not half so richly variegated o'er
The veil imperial that Esther wore,
When to the golden sceptre she drew nigh
To plead the cause of Judah doom'd to die;
Not half so exquisite that robe divine,
Of grace and second sanctity the sign,
Woven in beauty by the Lord of all
For our sweet Mother Eva at the Fall!

   This, then, as round her gracious form they
        drew,
Forth from its folds of interchanging hue
Odours of sacred myrrh and cassia stole;
Which through the good Franciscan's secret soul
Piercing far deeper than the pores of sight,
So fill'd his inmost being with delight,
That in their spiritual effluence rare
He seem'd of other worlds to drink the air,
And to himself beneath its potent sway
Appear'd as one dissolving all away!

CANTO VI.

La Corona.

O ENGLAND, which erewhile a peerless gem,
  Set in St. Peter's triple diadem,
So sparkledst, that the nations in amaze
Stood dazzled in the lustre of thy rays!
My Country! what a grief art thou to me,
Fallen from thine original majesty!
How oft, lamenting o'er thy sad career,
For thee, for thee, I pour the pensive tear,
And marvel at thy ignominious fate,
So holy once and excellently great!

Oh, medley of strange opposites combined!
Oh, wonder, envy, pity, of mankind!
So wise, so high; so ignorant, so base;
So rich in nature, and so poor in grace;
A land of truth, by fictions all depraved!
A land of freedom, to itself enslaved!
The lowest depth, alas, of all thy woe
So little thy true misery to know!

Ah, hadst thou only in a happier hour
More faithfully withstood the Tempter's power;
Nor meanly at an abject despot's nod
Forsworn thy Creed, and turn'd thee from thy God;
Not then, as now, the spoil of sense and time,
Shorn of ideas celestial and sublime,
Would thy whole life to ruin blindly go,
Pour'd on materialities below :
Not then, as now, unable to resume
Thy forfeit place in world-wide Christendom,
Wouldst thou in bitter isolation dwell,
Nursing within thy breast a secret Hell,
Which haply, soon or late, may burst amain
And rend thy growth of centuries in twain !

Oh, too unconscious of thy strange decay !
Didst thou but understand in this thy day
The things which, now to thee an idle song,
To thy true peace and truest life belong ;
With what a generous warmth wouldst thou receive
That message, which to scorn and disbelieve
Is now thy boast !   Ah ! ere it be too late,
Queen of the Isles ! reverse thy coming fate,
And recognise in thy misfancied foe
The Holy Church, sole healer of thy woe.

E'en now methinks, allured by Mary's prayer,
I see thee lend a less reluctant ear,
And, mindful of thy Faith's immortal home,
Turn a half-wistful glance to injured Rome!
E'en now I hear, in whispers borne around,
A yearning sigh for something more profound;
And mid thy discords catch a tone sublime
That seems the prelude of a better time!

Such tones on Euthanase's ear there fell
Soft-soothing; as the wonder-working spell
Of that fair flower of Avon in his hand
Recall'd him, wandering on Oblivion's strand.
For now a solemn pause announces all
Prepared;—and but some hand pontifical
Is needed, Heaven's own diadem to place
Upon that forehead of surpassing grace;
When plucking sharp his mantle's russet fold,
" They bring the Coronal! Behold, behold!"
His friend exclaims. He turn'd, and, through the
　　　　door
That from the Abbey-Cloister led of yore,
With waving lights, and chant reëcho'd clear
Antiphonally from the distant rear,

At the far end the Northern Transept down
Forth issues the Procession of the Crown.

Foremost of all, advancing grave along,
Of youthful priests a lovely shining throng,
With one, their leader, who on high before
The Instruments of Christ's dear Passion bore.
In snowy albs array'd, that swept the lawn,
And crimson stoles across their bosoms drawn,
Wands of victorious laurel in their hands,
Their foreheads filleted with myrtle bands,
Around each guileless head a nimbus bright
Weaving innocuous its golden light,
Serene in sweetest majesty they came
A blooming pageantry, and sang the Psalm
Of royal David—" Oh, how lovely shine
Thy Tabernacles, Lord of hosts divine!
My spirit faints away Thy Courts to see,
My flesh exults, O living God, in Thee!
Where hath the sparrow found himself a nest?
Here, Lord, within Thy Sanctuary blest;
Where spreads the turtle-dove her brooding wing?
Amidst thine altars, O my God and King!"

Of whom thus Theodore: " Ah! gaze thy fill,
And let this Heaven-imprinting spectacle

Sink in thy spirit's depth; for these are they,
The Seminary Priests—who in the day
Of false Elizabeth, and through the time
Of later-born apostasy and crime,
Confronting all the might of England's laws,
Stood up undauntedly in Faith's high cause,
And gloried by a traitor's death to die,
Battling against Satanic heresy!
For certain slaughter from the first prepared,
Like early victims for the altars rear'd,
Hunted, proscribed, in loathsome dungeons laid,
To all their kindred an opprobrium made,
Betray'd to death and torture,—bound in chains,
Hung,—disembowell'd amid cruel pains,
Their living hearts they offer'd to the Lord,
Torn from their bleeding breasts by hands
        abhorr'd;
And gave their blood, so miserably spilt,
In mediation for their country's guilt;
Too glad to pour their tender lives away
In the pure hope of England's better day!
Hail, Flowers of Martyrdom! hail, lovely band!.
Dear Intercessors of your native land!
Who for the love of God's eternal truth
Renounced the pleasant joyance of your youth,

Now foremost in the line that comes to set
On Mary's brow her mystic coronet!"

" Hail," Euthanase rejoins, " O Patriots blest!
But whence the halos which their brows invest?
On Saints beatified such honours wait,
But these were never raised to Saints' estate."

" Few only," thus the other in reply,
" Few only of the glorious Saints on high
On earth have honour, and for one below
The mansions of the skies a thousand show.
Yet the times come, and are not far away,
When yonder Blest shall see their Festal-day
In Britain's Isle, if right the signs I read,
And have of worship due their earthly meed ;
To them invoking throngs shall pour their sighs,
To them the dedicated temple rise !
And you, dear Saints, forgive the long delay,
Nor cease for your loved Albion to pray,
Till every hill and vale, from shore to shore,
Rings with the Angelus it heard of yore !"

Meanwhile, from forth his flower of Paradise,
That water-lily fair, began to rise

And through the Monk's more inward sense to pour
A keener, rarer odour than before;
As if to rally from its hidden source
With subtle searchings all his spirit's force
For what remain'd.   Anon there thrills a peal
Of music most inspired, ecstatical,
And forth appears the long coruscant line
Of England's Pontiff-Sanctities divine.

In Hierarchal order, See by See,
And all the pomp of sacred majesty,
Sublime they came, a marvel to behold,
Glory immortal of the days of old!
Each at his side a jewell'd crozier bore,
Each on his head a jewell'd mitre wore,
Each in august pontificals array'd
Honour and grace in all his mien display'd.
Of whom revolving, as they onward came,
To which in turn belong'd each sainted name
Of Pontiff blest, eternized in the page　　　·
Of England's history from age to age,
Thus Euthanase: " E'en such a mitred line,
Things earthly to compare with things divine,
These aged eyes beheld some while ago,
Within the Church yet Militant below,

Triumphant here.   For when, at Peter's call,
Our first high Synod met since England's fall,
Duly convened where central in the land
Mary beholds her own fair College stand,
(Five summers past, so quick the moments fly,
Just on the verge of this half century),
I too was there, the closing scene to view,
Marking well pleased our Hierarchy new
Around the cloisters wend with glad acclaim,
And joying to behold in England's realm
The basis firm, by that High Synod's aid,
Of order for the coming ages laid!"

"Ah, Euthanase, and could but then thy gaze
Have pierced mortality's enfolding haze,
There hadst thou seen," makes Theodore reply,
"How, in advance of that high Company,
Floated aloft in circumambient light
St. Michael, brandishing his sword of might;
The same that smote the Rebel Prince accursed,
With his apostate Spirits at the first.
For those were they, the honour of thy time,
Who come in Apostolic strength sublime,
For England's championship with Hell to fight,
And save her haply in her own despite,

Now in predestination's iron date
Nearing the secret crisis of her fate:
Whom to receive her greatness shall restore,
And raise her glory higher than before;
Whom to reject abandons her a prey
To ruin, loss, and infinite decay!
But, as I think, the Crown must now be near,
For see who strewing blossoms next appear!"

Thereat in purple mantles richly dight
Of boyish princes came a pageant bright;
Some with emblazon'd bannerets display'd
Symbolical of Heaven's unsullied Maid;
Others incessant scattering on their way
Pinkest and whitest tufts of spicy may,
So thick that scarce the floor of emerald green
For very snow of blossoms could be seen.
" Of Britain's kings the sainted youthful race
Ere yet she lost her heritage of grace!
Who leads the rest with our Salvation's Sign,
St. Kenelm, glory of old Mercia's line!"
Said Theodore. " All these as Martyrs died;
Or, Confessors of Christ, for regal pride
A cloister chose; or fell in pilgrimage;
Who might have been the glory of their age,

Had they so will'd; but they its glory fled,
And chose another glory in its stead:
Now with the Lamb they reign for ever His,
And share with Mary the abodes of bliss!
Oh, see upon each brow and beaming face
How shine baptismal innocence and grace!"

Then from within the Transept's depth of
    light
Began to dawn a brightness yet more bright,
So full, so rich, so luminous, so keen,
It seem'd they had till now in darkness been;
Brightness—yet such as dazzled not the eyes,
But with its roseate hues of Paradise
Rather infused in them new strength to see,
Participants of its own purity!
Forth from the Crown it stream'd, which borne
    along
Mid incense-wreaths and wafts of joyous song,
Now came in view. Upon a cushion white
Of downy plumes it lay, a lovely sight,
Thrilling the heart-strings by its presence blest
With a new sense of bliss before unguess'd.
A Heaven to see! But who of mortal birth
Might paint the sight? So little there of earth.

So much ethereal seem'd—a tracery rare
Alternately of rose and lily fair,
Lost in a mystery of spiry rays!—
So much to Euthanase a moment's gaze
Reveal'd; but when he strove with curious eye
Its more exact proportions to espy,
The clear empyreal texture undefiled
From that too earthly glance itself withheld,
And all a maze became—a maze of light
So purely and insufferably bright,
That nature reel'd, and reason from her throne
Seem'd on the instant headlong toppling down.
Inward he shrank, resolved to search no more;
And straightway all was lovely as before!

But who is he with such a glorious mien
That bears the Diadem of glory's Queen;
In England's old Regalia of state
A King array'd, magnificently great?
Already the Franciscan's heart had guess'd,—
Of England's monarchs greatest, wisest, best,
Edward the Confessor, his childhood's love,
Earliest of all his chosen Saints above.
Absorb'd in worship of that splendour fair
Which he so well had merited to bear;

G

His rich dalmatic floating to the ground,
His saintly retinue attendant round,
Serene he came, in every step a King,
While thus a thousand greeting voices sing:
" High glory to the Diadem divine,
Fabric immortal of the sacred Trine!
High glory to the Diadem divine,
Lady of grace, predestinated thine!
The Diadem prepared from endless days
In thy Immaculate Conception's praise;
No other crown so excellently fair,
No brow so fitted such a crown to wear!"

By this, the Pontiff Saints who went before
Had through the Abbey's Sanctuary-door
Enter'd the Choir, and there on either hand
Majestical in solemn order stand;
To whom nor blazon'd throne, nor altar fair,
For Coronation rite were wanting there;
Such change angelic ministries unseen
Had wrought on what had lately ruin been.
For where, before our holy Faith's decay
Rose the High Altar of an earlier day,
Long since by ruthless hands defaced, destroy'd,
And leaving in its stead a doleful void,

There now inlaid with gems of orient light
Another Altar stood superbly bright,
Surpassing all that fancy can invent
In symmetry and sculptured ornament;
So fair, so rich, so mystic to behold,
It seem'd as though that Altar of pure gold
Which glows upon the Heaven's translucent floor,
Circled with odorous incense evermore
Of saintly prayer, had left its upper realm,
And buoyant on the wings of Cherubim
Floated to earth!   Behind it, tier on tier,
A super-altar rose in beryl clear,
With golden candlesticks and flowers bedight,
In preparation for th' approaching rite;
While on its left, upon a dais green,
A vacant throne of amethyst is seen,
Lovelier than that which Solomon of old
Devised of ivory and finest gold.

Here, then, the Pontiff Majesties divine
On either side appear in solemn line,
Of whom, as now in clearer view they show,
Some Euthanase or knew or seem'd to know;
Aidan and Ninian among the rest;
St. Cuthbert and St. Swithun; Anselm blest;

St. Thomas, Canterbury's ancient pride,
Patron of England's clergy and their guide,
(He with his priests upon the Altar's right
As Celebrant stood forth in aureoled light);
St. Chad; St. Dunstan's majesty severe;
Wolstan and Osmund; Wilfrid ever dear.
Such in appearance as at boyhood's dawn
Their figures oft in fancy he had drawn,
Musing o'er Butler's monitory page
Beneath the murmurous summer foliage,
So in resemblance now they met his sight,
The same in countenance and form and height.
Save only that more glorious they seem'd
Than ever thought conceived or fancy dream'd!

   Thus as he notes, a merry pealing chime
Rings out as in the Abbey's olden time;
And up the choir the Diadem is borne,
Glittering resplendent as the star of morn,
On bended knee received with reverence due,
And on the Altar laid in open view.

CANTO VII.

Finale.

NOW in their contemplation of the Grace
Which lifted Thee so far above thy race,
And set Thee, Lady, in ethereal light
On Thy Immaculate Conception's height,
'Twas wondrous how that Saintly Company
To Thy fair circlet turn'd admiringly,
Lost in adoring depths of joy divine,
To see the Heaven-created mystic Sign
Of that high Privilege ordain'd above
In preparation for Incarnate Love,
Inauguration of th' eternal plan
That links with God regenerated man!
Long was their gaze—one act of worship all,
Solemn, subdued, intense, ecstatical!
As though in that dear Mystery's abyss
Their meditation found such store of bliss,
That powerless th' attraction to dissever,
It there must dwell for ever and for ever!

Meanwhile o'er all around with deep'ning spell
A rapture of expectant silence fell,
If silence might be call'd what rather were
A sacred super-silence born of prayer;
A breath of Heaven; a Heaven-inbreathing power;
Such silence as befel in that half hour
Th' Apocalypse records—a blissful sea
Of imperturbable tranquillity
In-flowing broad and deep; whereon upborne
Our Euthanase beyond the gates of morn
Floated in spirit Heavenward;—when, lo!
A stir—a solemn movement to and fro;
And as in beauty peers the rising moon
Above the cedar-tops of Lebanon;
Or as the flowery exhalations glide
In balmy mist along by Carmel's side;
Or as in some fair garden of delights,
Full of entrancing sounds and scents and sights,
Forth from a lily-bank you should behold
A bird of Paradise its plumes unfold;
So from amidst her ring of virgins fair
Our Lady rose, an odoriferous air
Breathing around, and through the bending
      throng
Betwixt her two Apostles glides along

To th' Altar floor.   There on th' Epistle side
Kneels in her beauty down the Heavenly Bride,
Fronting the Celebrant, and gives to sight
(Sideways she knelt, the Altar on her right,)
That type of absolute Virginity
Sedate in intellectual majesty,
Worshipp'd by all the Cherubim!—her face
In adoration rapt; a golden grace
Of lustrous locks upon her shoulders strown;
Her arms across her bosom meekly drawn,
As though in sweetness of humility
Herself resigning to the dignity
She might not shun—a Vision exquisite
Of perfect Maidenhood, wherein were met,
From touch of earth etherealised, refined,
As in some pure abstraction of the mind,
All honour, beauty, virtue, tenderness;
All wisdom, modesty, and graciousness;
All love, all joy, all truth and constancy,
Blended in calm repose and unity!
Such vision as to Raphael's longing eyes
Ne'er came in dreams of morn from Para-
        dise;
Such vision as ne'er thrill'd Correggio,
Nor Guido, nor the blest Angelico;

Once only by Murillo caught in part,
And lost again, ere glowing from the heart
His canvas had received its image rare;
Though e'en as such it lives for ever there!

Thus as she knelt, the Celebrant divine
Down from the Altar took the mystic Sign
Of grace original and glory bright.
Inestimable Diadem of light;
And tracing with it in exultant wave
The Cross on high, first reverently gave
A Benediction round; then on the brow
So alabaster white upturn'd below,
The lovely Radiance laid.   Forthwith a strain
Of jubilant hosannas bursts amain,
In acclamations glad; and from her knees
Uprising amidst heavenly harmonies,
Our Lady to her amethystine throne
Amidst her saintly splendours passes on;
And so with ceremonious rites complete
Assumes, endiadem'd, her glory-seat.

There as she sate enthroned triumphantly
In brightness of unblemish'd majesty,
Forth steps Britannia's kingly Confessor,
Who in his jewell'd hand resplendent bore

A Sceptre fair. Not half so fair the Rod
Of Aaron bloom'd before the Ark of God,
Discovering to enraptured Israel's sight
Its budding growth of almond-blossoms bright,
As this its opal stem exposed to view
Floriferous with gems of heavenly hue;
While at the top, in softly-feather'd rays,
The emblematic Dove its form displays.

This bearing then he knelt at Mary's feet;
And royally in words of homage meet
(So Euthanase or heard or seem'd to hear,
A mystery the whole to eye and ear),
Presented it. "O Virgin Glory, deign
To take this Sceptre of our Isle again:
For Thee reserved through melancholy years,
For Thee through martyrdoms of blood and tears,
Long under seas of persecution toss'd,
Obscure it lay, and seem'd for ever lost.
Now with the dawning of a better time,
Reflourishing more fair than at its prime,
Again returns. O Virgin Queen, to Thee
This symbol of thine early sovereignty!
Oh, take it back, and by its gentle sway
For happy days to come ordain the way.

Defend the Hierarchy; crush, subdue
The strength of Heresy; prepare anew
A people for the Lord, and by their aid
Illuminate the lands in darkness laid,
Till earth's far ends a thousandfold restore
For all that England lost to Heaven of yore!"

He ceased; but She a moment's space delay'd,
As one by hidden cause uncertain made,
A moment lifted an adoring eye
To gather inspiration from on high,
Then courteous bent, and with a smiling face,
Into her hand received the pledge of grace.

Whereof as Euthanase th' interior sense
Drank in with contemplative gaze intense,
The other thus: "Alas, that word of mine
Should interrupt, dear friend, thy joy divine!
But here the rite concludes. See all around
Stir of departure!" Saying this he wound
An arm in his; and with obeisance paid
To Heaven's encoronall'd and sceptred Maid,
Him lingering, and with all his spirit's might
Clinging to that fair Vision of delight,
Led out upon the mead.—The mounted sun
Full in its clear meridian brightness shone;

Yet dimmer all around the prospect lay
To eyes so late immersed in heavenly day,
Than when, O Tintern, o'er thine ivied walls
Through night's dim vault the trickling starlight
      falls !

But they by orchard sweet, and wicket door,
And cloister wall, the way they pass'd before,
Sped silent back ; till on the river bank
Forth stepping, lo ! before them, rank in rank
With harpers fill'd, a Roman galley rode,
Its beak directed down the ebbing flood.
Harpstrings and harps reflected in the stream,
Glister'd again, but so their golden gleam
To Euthanase as though the midnight moon
Upon thy bosom, Wye, were floating down !

To whom thus Theodore : " O, Ancients, say
To what sea-bordering shrine you speed your
      way ?"
When one in answer : " To St. Tecla's Isle ;
Ye also in our galley, if ye will."
Thus as he spoke, the golden-crested prow
Up to the marge he urged, whereon they two
Were standing side by side ; and entering straight
Downwards they thread the mazes intricate

Of sylvan waters fair.   No faintest cloud
Obscured the sky, and on the moving flood
A summer sunshine lay; but all around
To Euthanase was still in twilight bound,
As when the pale Aurora's early ray
First trembling breaks along the edge of day !

Thus gliding down betwixt the wooded hills,
A tide of countless thoughts his bosom fills,
In ebb and flow; and mingling with them all
An inner sense of joy ecstatical,
To think our Lady took that Sceptre bright,
To think that England yet, in Hell's despite,
May live to God.   But of the times and end,
Dubious : " Oh, say," he cries, " celestial friend,
How shall it be, and when ?   So many years
Pass onward, and so distant still appears
Our boyhood's hope."   Then he : " Too oft the plan
Of loving grace is shorn by stubborn man
Of its full issue; yet of this be sure,
And in the happy prospect rest secure,
Again shall Britain in her greater part
Return to God, and welcome to her heart
The Faith so long abjured ; so much to me
Cedmon disclosed in solemn prophecy,—

Cedmon, of Saxon minstrels first and best,
St. Hilda's poet-herdsman ever-blest!
For, seated lately on the sapphire skies
At watch with him, while underneath our
      eyes
This ocean gem its landscape fair unroll'd,
I ask'd of him to sing, as once of old
In Hilda's hall Creation's tale he sang
To wondering ears.   And he at first began
As I desired; but, shifting by degrees,
His strain to England turn'd, and mysteries
Of England's coming time;—and I who heard,
Part understood, and part from part inferr'd,
And part in darkness left, as unto me
Inscrutable.   But, oh! what times shall be,
If rightly I interpreted his song!
For of a change he sang, and troubles long;
Of clashing armaments, and carnage sore;
And horrid wars exceeding all before;
Famine and Pestilence, Invasion dire;
Cities far inland wrapt in hostile fire!
Democracy against a tottering throne
Breaking in seas of blood;—nor these alone,
But other evils born of social crime,
And battening on the miseries of the time!

Then—in the midst of all—when hope is fled,
And England bows to God her humbled head,
Comes Mercy from on high, and in her train
Come Order, Truth, and Liberty again;
Comes Justice, and time-honour'd majesty
Of sceptred kings!—But when a king shall be
Sprung from Victoria's imperial line,
Who for the Faith his sceptre shall resign,
And at his people's prayer the same resume
Purged from ancestral taint and clinging doom
Of heresy;—then, Britain, hail the time,
For then returns thy blissful golden prime;
Then long-expected Arthur reigns anew,
Thy Saint and King to come, who shall sub-
      due
All hearts, and blend in unity again
The broken links of thy historic chain.
He to the See of Peter shall restore
The Isle of Saints, and closer than before
Their union knit. The Churches of the land,
The Minsters that in hoar oblivion stand,
The sacred Abbeys desolate so long,
He to the Faith with Sacrifice and song
Shall open; so re-opened to remain,
Until the Lord of glory comes again.

Peace and all plenty in his reign shall be;
And Arts unguess'd; and Science as a sea
Expanding wide, no more with Faith at war;
And Glory such as England never saw
At her superbest height; and exercise
Of Heaven-born Charity: and when he dies,
All Christendom shall canonise his name,
And place it in her topmost roll of fame.
But who shall live these miracles to see?—
Pray thou at least that of this Prophecy
God to our Isle more gracious than her meed
The evil part abridge, the happier speed!"

Thus as he spoke, there seem'd a rippling strange,
The prelude indistinct of coming change,
To flutter o'er our Euthanase's mind,
Breaking its mirror clear; as when a wind
Breathes o'er a lake which quiet hills enclose,
Disturbing from their picture-like repose
Its nether anti-type of earth and skies;
Conscious of which, "O Theodore," he cries,
"Let us not part; but by the friendship fond
That made us one in boyhood's early bond,
If, as I guess, with those Three Children fair
To Glastonbury's courts you next repair,

Me also take."   A sudden half-drawn sigh,
Unless it were a zephyr whispering by,
Gave Theodore.   " Ah, dearest," he replied,
" Were mine the choice, nought should again divide
Our constant hearts ; but, oh ! it may not be,
If rightly bodes mine inward augury.
Yet fear thee not : for safe from every harm,
And lapp'd by mystic harpings in the calm
Of some deep-soothing and Elysian dream,
This bark shall bear thee up Sabrina's stream,
To Mary's Wood.   There hands shall interlace,
And lift thee up, and softly to the place
Transport thee with melodious lullaby
Where first thou didst our pageantry espy.
Thus parting here, upon th' eternal shore
Soon meet we, brother best, to part no more !"

    By this, through craggy clefts of woodland high,
Tracing the sinuous outlet of the Wye,
Past Chepstow they had sped ; and now they steer
To Tecla's hallow'd Isle more slowly near,
When Theodore within a fond embrace
Enfolding fast his weeping Euthanase,
Ere yet th' approaching keel had grazed the strand,
Leap'd light ashore, and with a waving hand

Sign'd to proceed.   The rowers straight obey,
And up the Severn waters turn their way.

But Euthanase;—upon the bark he stood
Irresolute, by tender thoughts subdued,
And gazed upon his friend;—so near to view,
And yet, oh, wonder strange! so distant too!
So near,—for scarce as yet a pebble's throw
Parts from the shore the slow-receding prow;
So far,—for in the flood that roll'd between
Eternity appear'd to intervene!
Transfix'd he gazed; his inmost vitals yearn;
He beckons to his beckoning friend in turn,
And forward strains.   That instant from his hold
Dropp'd the white Lily with the crest of gold,
And on the dancing tide was borne away
Twinkling alternate with the twinkling spray!
He watch'd it drifting o'er the wavelets fleet;
He watch'd it—till it rested at the feet
Of Theodore, who stooping caught it up
And waved it thrice, and kiss'd its pearly cup,
And to his bosom the fair token drew
Expressively, and look'd a last adieu!

H

FROM morn to noon, from noon to twilight gray,
Calmly in Mary's Wood had sped the day,
Since first upon the old Franciscan's sight
Down the green alley stole that Vision bright;
No footfall there, nor busy sound had been,
To break the quiet of the sylvan scene.
On into eve the fading twilight wore;
Night follow'd, closing fast her ebon door;
Forth came the stars upon the deep'ning sky;
And hush'd was all the woodland symphony,
Save when the skirts of some low-trailing breeze
Just stirr'd the topmost summits of the trees,
Or from her secret arbour warbled clear
The bird of melody in midnight's ear.

But when again a new Aurora broke,
And all the sleeping grove to life awoke;
When the fresh diamonds bestrew'd the lawn,
And countless wood-notes welcomed in the dawn:
Then as the Monastery brothers go
In search of their dear Father to and fro,
So many hours now missing from his home
Since forth he took the blest Viaticum,

Lo! where, as centre of the winding ways,
A gray Druidic stone its form displays,
Him motionless upon his knees they spy,
Lost seemingly in some deep ecstasy.
Softly they step, as fearing to intrude
Too harshly on that sacred solitude;
Till, now more near, they find their Father dead,
The form indeed erect, the spirit fled!

There on the selfsame spot, where first he view'd
The golden-glistening Pageant of the Wood,
Supported by the stone, he rested still,
His rosary betwixt his fingers chill;
His arms across each other meekly press'd
Clasping the Sacred Presence to his breast;
Upon his face a smile most heavenly fair,
As having gain'd, according to his prayer,
That guerdon from the Majesty on high,
In Heaven's best time a happy death to die!

THE MINSTER OF ELD.

MINSTER OF ELD! in thy sweet solemn shade
   How pleasant is it thus apart to roam!
Here for myself a shelter I have made;
   In thee my pilgrim spirit finds a home.
Hither withdrawing from the day's false glare,
   From earthliness and all that breeds annoy,
She hath wrought out a resting-place from care,
   And drinks unwatch'd from hidden fount of
        joy;
Oh, cruel world that can such happiness destroy!
   For while in quiet thought I wander on,
      Those peaceful courts along,
      Too oft its clangours sound
   And jar the golden chords so finely strung
      On which my soul had hung;
   Then sinks the Minster in a depth profound,
      And alone I seem to stand
      On some disenchanted land,
      Lost upon a desert drear,
      All a blank to eye and ear,
      Seeking ofttimes long in vain
      Ere I can return again.

      Ah me! what time hath pass'd
      Since here I enter'd last!

Almost I seem a stranger here to be,
As though no right I had mine own dear halls to see!
　　　Oh, archetypal Place!
　　　Pure mystery of space!
　　　Which, as my glance around I throw,
　　　Dost into clearer outline grow.
　　　Oh, music that above me sweeps
　　　Like anthem of uplifted deeps!
　　　Oh, roof of roofs sublime,
　　　Wrought in the world's young prime!
　　　Oh, pillars firm, that seem
　　　More vast than thought may dream!
　　　Oh, lights and shades that fall
　　　So strange and mystical,
　　　Slanting from wall to wall!
　　　Oh, tints most rare!
　　　Oh, gently-breathing air!
　　　Oh, floor so green and fair!
　　　　　Here let me dwell,
　　　Choosing some holy cell;
　　　　　Here let me sing
　　　To solemn-sounding string,
　　　Thy works, my God and King!
　　　Joying with all creation to proclaim
　　　For ever the high glory of thy Name!

THE MINSTER OF ELD.

Interior of a vast Minster.

PILGRIM.

WAS it a fancy, or in very truth
    Did I behold angelic faces near me?
And there was music too! It is most strange;
Once in my boyhood's morn I had a dream
Of a most noble Minster, rear'd aloft
Upon the realms of Chaos and old Night,
Fair in proportion, full of mysteries,
And typical of all creation's scheme;
A supernatural glorious edifice
Raised by no hand of mortal architect!
Most curiously it dwelt upon my mind,
And, as I grew, supplied to teeming fancy
A subtle food, and to myself I named it
Minster of Eld! Now in its very courts

I seem to be, how hither brought at all
From couch of weary convalescence long,
A secret unexplain'd; and as I gaze,
Unless my sense deceive, it spreads abroad
Wider and wider still its beauteous aisles.
How pleasant is this turf, with fairy-rings
Of old primeval growth! How delicate
The scent of flowering thyme, which as I tread
I cannot choose but crush! This door that stands
As entrance to the Nave, is broad and high
Beyond imagination, yet not larger
Than suits the rest; and yonder seven great
              bolts
That keep it closed in bonds of adamant,
Writ o'er with hieroglyphics mystical,
So massive seem, they well might typify
The very bars of Nature which hold fast
The Universe in one! Upon the seventh
Appears a Roman text, which may afford
Haply some clue to my perplexity.

                           [*He reads.*

    " When the Universe was made,
      On its hinge this door was laid;
      Once unbolted hath it been;
      Once again shall so be seen.

When its folds were opened first,
Inward the flood of waters burst;
When they next apart shall leap,
Inward a flood of flame shall sweep.
In the midst of that great din
Comes the King of glory in,
He who at Creation's door
Watching standeth evermore!"

Methinks I can decipher me in part
The meaning here contain'd.   Oh, joy of joys!
And can it then be so in very deed
As I somewhile have thought, that here I stand
Within that glorious Minster of old time,
    Which in my boyhood's days
Did evermore around me seem to rise,
    By glimpses caught through the half-open-
            ing haze
Of Nature's outward mutabilities,
  Then quick withdrawn again, lest I
  Within its secret aisles too eagerly should
            pry.
        Oh, Minster of my youth,
        How oft on mossy stone
            Seated alone

In the deep woods I heard thine anthem's solemn
tone!
How oft I saw unfold
Around the setting sun thy skirts of gold,
And felt mine inmost heart dance with a joy un-
told!
And of thy glories to imbibe did seem,
Till thou alone wast real and earth a dream!

Brief date had those glad hours,
Soon by advancing manhood put to flight;
The world with all its powers
Came sweeping on before my ravish'd sight,
And I with it was borne, as on the waves of
night,
Far from sweet Nature's face,
Too far, my God, from Thee and thine embrace,
Till the fair vision of mine earlier years
Faded in mists of tears,
And its sweet music found no echo in mine ears!
Thrice welcome then, blest place,
If so indeed it be,
Up whose long avenues with joy I go;
And may thy scenes efface
Henceforth for me

Remembrance of vile earthly things below,
Which all too long endures, feeding the heart with
        woe.

                [He proceeds up the aisle.

How soft and pearly is the light that doth
Inhabit here! Yon pillars, dimly shown
Through swathing clouds, might vie in girth and
        height
With Babel's Tower. This floor is one vast down,
On which a thousand herds might feed apart
And still leave room for more.   But, as I see,
On yonder mound there sits a shepherd-boy
Beside his nibbling flock. I will address him.
What, ho! good shepherd boy, canst tell me
        aught
About this holy fane?

SHEPHERD BOY.

             Nay, Sir, not much
Myself, but not so far away there dwells
A Hermit of Mount Carmel, who will tell thee
All thou canst wish to learn. If thou art thirsty,
Here is a most sweet spring; and I entreat thee
Take bread from my poor scrip. Oh, I have seen
Strange things upon the plain since I came hither
To keep this flock in charge. The Angel Choirs,

The same that sang in Bethlehem,—oft I've heard
Singing o'erhead in the still moonlight hour.
If thou wilt go with me, I'll show the way
To where the Hermit lives.   But I must call
My sister first, now absent gathering lilies
To weave a necklace for some favourite
Amongst her lambkins.   She will hasten back
Soon as she hears this pipe.

                    [He plays, and they proceed together.

SCENE II.

An open plain in the nave.

PILGRIM.

We have been stepping fast, and must have come
A league upon our way.

SHEPHERD BOY.

                  'Tis difficult,
I've noticed, to judge here of distances.
What seem'd remote but now, being often found
At hand when least expected; what seem'd near
In turn far off; such mystery there is
In all that to this Minster appertains.

PILGRIM.

I have observed it too; and had ascribed it
To some rare trick of fancy.   But, behold,
The curtain of the mist is lifting up
Its heavy folds, and shows the massive pillars
Clear to their base; the windows, or what may
To windows correspond, begin to cast
Through their diminish'd cloudy drapery
A rainbow tint; and a suffusèd purple
Has gather'd overhead; while far away
Yon screen its range of crested pinnacles
Shows like an alabaster glacier
Betwixt two mountains piled!

                                  [*Music.*

                  Ah! what a strain
Of harmony was there!   Never before
Heard I such music.   Hark! it swells again
And rains down like a shower.

SHEPHERD BOY.

                  There are strange harps,
Let down at intervals by golden threads,
Along the aisles, whence spring these gracious
                sounds,
As it would seem, spontaneous.   Come this way.

And I will show thee one.   Lo! where it hangs;
Would it were low enough for thee to touch!

PILGRIM.

O beauteous Instrument!   O Harp of eld!
What symmetry it hath, resembling those
Of th' ancient Druids! with a hoary moss
Of silver sprouting on its delicate frame!
But for the present mute!

SHEPHERD BOY.

                         It will begin
To sound again, if we but wait.   I see
Already a vibration in the chords.   •
         [It sounds, gradually increasing in depth
                  and variety.

PILGRIM.

Oh, miracle of tones! oh, most divine
Capacity in instrument so slight!
Or is it rather that the music flows
Not from the chords themselves, but from the stir
Which by some deep affinity they work
In other unsuspected influences?
It must be so.   For now it sounds afar,
Now near, now all around, in height and depth

Ascending and descending through the scales
Of such a multitudinous harmony,
As though within itself it did embrace
All the wide compass of creation's tones.
Now 'tis the tinkling of a shower—and now
The whistling wind—anon the solemn roll
Of mountain waves, changing by slow degrees
To muttering thunder. Oh, I could stay and listen
For ever to the ever-varying strain,
So jubilant awhile; and then so sad,
Enough to melt the very soul away
With its deep hidden pathos!

SHEPHERD BOY.

                              I have heard,
The tones of jubilation are the praise
Which Nature pays her Lord; the sad her moans
For her own fall in Adam, mix'd with yearnings
For the great Day of Restitution,
When all things shall in Christ be made anew.
But see the spot where dwells the holy Hermit
I told thee of!

PILGRIM.

                          I see it: a long range
Of curious cells scoop'd in the solid rock,

I

With immemorial ivy over-brow'd;
In front a sloping sward, on which appears
A broken altar of th' old Pagan time,
If right I guess.

SHEPHERD BOY.

Here, then, I leave thee, Pilgrim;
My task complete: God's blessing rest on thee!
[*Exit.*

SCENE III.

Front of a Hermitage. The Hermit is seen carving a Crucifix on the rock.

HERMIT.

Another touch might mar it.   Holy Christ,
Who so for me didst die on Calvary,
Accept this dear memorial of thy love,
Which here upon my knees I dedicate
To th' everlasting glory of thy Name.

PILGRIM, *entering.*

Forgive me, holy Hermit, breaking thus
Upon thy solitude.   A shepherd boy
Guided me here to thee, as one who might

Resolve for me the meaning of this place.
                    [*Observing the Crucifix.*
() work of grace!   What glorious majesty
Sits on the brow, with depth of patient grief
Divinely mingled!   Wonders have I seen
Of art, but none like this.

HERMIT.

                         No art is here
But that of love and contemplation ;
A longer gaze would show thee sore defects
In what at present pleases.   'Tis the work
Of hands most rude and inexperienced.
But if concerning this our Minster here
Knowledge thou seek, I have some certain Rhymes
Which to the Pilgrims who go by this way
Sometimes I do rehearse: these will I now
Recite to thee, as best my memory serves ;
We sitting by yon altar-step the while.
                    [*They approach the altar.*

PILGRIM.

This altar hath most excellent proportions,
Ionic in its style, and, as 'twould seem,
Of purest Parian.   Pity that 'tis rent
As by some shock of sudden violence.

Its dedication still is legible
In Greek: " TO THE UNKNOWN GOD."

HERMIT.

This neighbourhood
The Pagans of old time did much frequent,
Such as with hearts sincere, in nature's works
Felt after nature's omnipresent God,
If haply they might find Him.   These were they
Who first began to scoop these hermitages.
This altar was their making.   Here with rites
Of solemn patriarchal sacrifice,
Confused with errors of strange ignorance,
Did they adore the Almighty Architect,
Their God unknown, yearning for clearer light
Of Revelation's dawn, as yet withheld:
Later there came the Christian anchorites,
And multiplied the cells, as now you see.

PILGRIM.

And this deep-fissured rent;—how came it thus?

HERMIT.

It is believed that when our Saviour died,
That earthquake, which upheaved the sepulchres,
Ran also through this Minster in its course.

And, among other traces, left behind
This shatter'd altar.

PILGRIM.

                        There is a pleasant moss
Upon the side that looketh to the East;
Here let us sit.   It hath grown visibly lighter
Since I was in the Minster, and the mist
Hath much dispersed.   How most majestically
Doth yonder neighbouring pillar lift its height,
So vast it scarcely seems to be a pillar,
And in comparison these cells in the rock
Appear to be no bigger than the holes
Of the sand-martin!   I saw Staffa once,
And marvell'd; but a thousand Staffas here,
Ascending from basaltic height to height,
Seem piled upon each other without end.
Yonder, across the plain, on the other side
Of the broad Nave, a solemn Porch appears,
Between which and the Transept I can count
The huge Titanic figured capitals
Of twenty several pillars, peering forth
Through their thin strata of aërial cloud,
As in the Pyrenees the crested peaks
At morning-tide.   But I am quite forgetting,

Lost in the mighty majesty around,
Thy promise, hoary-headed Solitary,
Me to instruct in its deep mysteries.

HERMIT.

O thou, who of this transcendental place
Seekest from me the origin to trace,
Know that, coëval with the earth and skies,
No less it dates than from creation's rise:
Such the tradition which through ages deep
Among themselves its angel-watchers keep.

For when, according to the eternal plan,
The universe from nothing first began,
All elements uniting in His name
Him to adore and bless from whom they came,
Straightway, as from the strings the music flows,
From their rich harmony this Temple rose,
An emanation from the things we see
Unto His praise, who caused them so to be.

To this great Minster, eldest-born of time,
Earth gave a floor, the heavens a roof sublime,
For pillars firm their heights the mountains rear'd,
And windows in the opening clouds appear'd,

The stars for lamps themselves in order rang'd,
The winds, into a glorious organ changed,
Chanted from side to side with solemn roar,
The waves from ocean and the woods from shore.

This Temple from the first hath standing been,
Open to all, yet evermore unseen,
Except by such as with a lowly mind
Sought in His loving works their God to find,
To whom, the more they gazed with reverence
            due,
More and more visible its glories grew;
While ever from the eyes that peer'd in pride
The structure, of itself, itself would hide.
But ceaselessly its solemn aisles along
Wander'd of angels bright a glorious throng,
Delighted that exuberance to behold
Of ever-flowing wonders new and old.

Now of this Minster if thou next desire
The form and heavenly pattern to inquire,
Know, that when early in the dawn of days
The Son made all things to the Father's praise,
Of His own Cross the everlasting sign
He stamp'd within Creation's depth divine,

Crosswise uprearing on th' abyss of space
The world whose scheme thou here dost dimly
                            trace:
Thus at the first in Eden we behold
Crosswise four rivers blend their sands of gold.
And still the Cross this Minster doth divide,
For all things draw towards the Crucified.

  Fourfold expands itself the glorious Fane
In Nave, and Choir, and mighty Transepts twain;
Each with its cloistral haunts, and chantries fair,
Each with its solemn aisles for praise and prayer,
And maze of inner windings half-unknown
E'en to the Seraphs that stand round the throne:
But if in all such countless courts are found,
Such grandeurs of creative love abound,
Still more the Choir excels the other three
In supernatural grace and majesty.

  Learn then, fast shut within Creation's shrine,
A place there is, part human part divine,
Made from the first by Him who set the spheres,
But open'd later in the midst of years
By Him again, when stooping from His throne
He drew our human life into His own.

Behind yon screen it lies, the portion blest
Of Holy Church, secluded from the rest.
Oh, place most dear, who can thy joys express,
Or paint the beauties of thy loveliness?
Oh, place most calm, who can thy shades forget,
Where only God's true Israel may be met?
Where dwelleth Faith in undisturb'd repose,
Where Hope and Charity their sweets disclose,
And all our earthly troubles vanish quite
In the Communion of the Saints in light!

Thus of this holy Temple, as I could,
I've traced for thee, my son, an outline rude;
More wonders still within its depths there be,
A boundless and unfathomable sea;
Some for thyself of these thou shalt explore,
And some shalt never know for evermore.

What else remains but His great Name to bless;
Him, Father, Son, and Spirit, to confess,
Who all things made by His eternal will,
Who all things by the same upholdeth still;
All things shall once again in ruin pour,
All things again shall once for all restore:
To Him be glory, praise, as in all time before!

PILGRIM.

Thanks, kind Interpreter; I now begin
Better to comprehend the great design
Unfolding all around: yet, oh, forgive,
If of yon Porch which in the distance shows
So vast and dim, unnoticed in thy Rhyme,
I dare to make of thee inquiry brief,
Touch'd with a strange and growing interest,
Whither it leads, what comes or goes thereby.

HERMIT.

Know, Pilgrim, then, besides the Western door,
Thou sawest first, the Minster hath two gates,
Which, opening out upon th' unseen abyss,
Entrance the one, the other exit gives
To nature's forms.   Within the Nave they stand,
Facing each other, and to each its Porch
Attach'd of old; whereof the one is named
The Porch of Life, for thereby entrance find
Organic things in their predestined mould
Into the world of sense; its opposite,
The Porch of Death, and thither all again
They tend; for, coming forth from the unknown,
And having wrought, each in its several shape,
Its task assign'd, straightway they onward go

Through Death's dread Portal to the gulf again.
Yonder it looms, so drear and shadowy,
Before thy very gaze!

PILGRIM.

       Ah, even here
Methinks I feel its chilly influence.
And now, as I remember me again
Of that sharp fever which I had of late
Nigh unto death, and of the wanderings strange
  Wherein my soul was borne;
Within myself I seem to recognise
  That I to that same Porch
  In spirit was led on
  By Sickness, vision pale;
And in the solemn vestibule did stand,
  And there half-open'd spied
  The unrelenting door;
And felt the outer air from the abyss
  Breathe coldly on my cheek;
  And in the dimness saw,
Where all amid the ever-vanishing crowd
Death solitary sate, wrapt in his sable shroud.
  Ah, then my foot
  Had all but slipp'd,

Its footing lost and gone,
And I unto myself had said :
' The world's inhabitants
No more shall I behold,
Nor Nature's gladsome brow.'
But One to me did reach his hand,
And drew me back to light and life again,
That I might better serve Him, so to win
His pardoning grace before I pass away.
    Now of that other Porch,
The Porch of Life, I fain would something know,
    For it I have not seen.

HERMIT.

              Thou sawest once
And passedst through it, but rememberest not,
For it was in thy newborn infancy ;
A wondrous spot, the womb of all that lives,
Upon this Southern side its station is,
    Beyond our present view :
    No blasts of winter there
        Chilling the air ;
No darkness dwells, nor spectral forms are seen,
But evermore an atmosphere serene
Thrills on the sense; and a strange stir of joy

Admitting naught that grieves,
Prevails, as of unnumber'd opening leaves
In a warm hour of April's sunshine coy,
  While Hope for ever guards the gate,
  And Angels of the Morn attendant wait.

PILGRIM.

Oh, Hermit blest,
But I would yet one question ask,
  If me thou wilt not chide.
  Lo! now from Death's dread Gate
  Granted for once reprieve,
Too certainly I know the day draws nigh
When I a second time must thither go,
  And back return no more,
But onward wend across the solemn sea,
Whose other shore is our eternal land.
  Then in the formless deep
  Plunging without a hold
  On aught to nature known,
  What may my soul betide
  Immortal borne along,
Ofttimes I shuddering meditate,
Conscious of ill desert and fill'd with fears un-
          told.

Oh, say if there be not some other door
   Whereby we may go forth
   And find a surer way
Across the illimitable dim profound ?

HERMIT.

Thou speakest well ; such door indeed there is ;
   But in the Choir it stands,
   Far distant from this spot,
Upon the further side of yonder screen,
Within the Lady Chapel, at the back
Of the High Altar.   A postern-gate it is
Of pearly semblance, and once open'd leads
Right up the crystal stair that spans th' abyss
   To happy Eden climes.
   But so withdrawn it lies,
That many pass thereby and see it not.
And long must mortal strive and patient wait,
   If he would entrance gain ;
Moreover, though the door was in its place
   Since first this Minster rose,
     Yet only late
Hath it to human effort open'd been ;
   For ever since the Fall
Closed it remain'd by double bolts outside,

Which none might draw, there being no way
          thither
    Save by a circuit long,
    First through the Gate of Death,
And then all round, coasting the outer edge
    Of the great Minster wall,
    Till to the back ye came;
    And this no man might do:
For each no sooner pass'd the gate of death
    Than down at once he sank
    In the sheer nameless depth,
Quite impotent upon the void to tread;
Therefore long time the pearly door was closed.
    Yet by tradition in part,
In part by instinct, to lost Adam's race
    The secret stair was known,
    And whither it led up.
    This prompted men to search,
    And many were the schemes
Which fancy or philosophy devised,
Or round the gulf to pass and draw the bolts,
    Or else the gate to force,
Or through the wall to cleave some other way.
    But all in vain was tried;
To Heaven's high palaces no path was found,

Until Emmanuel came,
Predicted of our race,
Of Virgin Mother born,
Mighty in word and deed,
Prince and High-Priest and Sacrifice in one.
He of his own accord
Did through the grave and gate of death proceed.
And entering on the void,
Trod with firm foot th' unsearchable abyss,
As on the sea of Galilee before;
Till passing round, up to that door He came,
To th' hinder part, and there both bolts withdrew.
Opening the way of everlasting life
Thenceforth to mortal man!
Oh, day of victory!
How with triumphant notes
This Minster did resound!
What music then was heard through earth and
Heaven!
Sweeter by far than at Creation's dawn,
When all the morning stars sang out for joy!

PILGRIM, *bowing his head.*

All praise to Him who wrought this wondrous
work,

At price of his own Blood.   Oh, lead me on,
   That I at once that heavenly door may see,
That stair may climb, and fleet away
   From earth without delay
To the clear realms of immortality.

HERMIT.

Thy time is not as yet.   The Lord hath work
For thee below.   O Pilgrim, here we part;
But let these words sink in thine inmost heart:
   If thou that door wouldst see
   Open itself to thee,
Long must thou toil, and patient must thou be,
   And bended oft thy knee;
Confiding still in nothing of thine own
But in the grace of thy dear God alone.

FAREWELL, a long farewell, O Minster green,
   Dim haunt of olden time!
Where with our Pilgrim I have wandering been;—
   Thou in thy strength sublime
Shalt still abide; nor be by me forgot,
Though, veil'd from earthly sense, I see thee not.

K

Thee oft the gather'd clouds reposing
Over the sunset's crimson closing,
Thee oft the forest aisle to mind shall bring;
 Of thee the mossy cell
 In lonely woodland dell,
 Of thee the winds shall tell,
 Of thee the budding Spring!
 Thy front of gold
Through the faint flush of morn I shall behold;
 Thy chant shall hear in ocean's roar
 Still echoing on for evermore!

Now to Him who all hath made
Everlasting praise be paid.
The time for Him it draweth near
In his own Temple to appear:
All Creation shall be dumb
When in His glory He shall come.
Who then may stand His face to see!
In that day, Jesu, pity me!

MISCELLANEOUS PIECES.

THE HOLY CATHOLIC CHURCH.

HOLY Church Catholic! Joy of the earth,
  In whom the nations have had a new birth!
Bond of the universe, binding in one
All the wide continents under the sun!
All believers, afar and near,
Who adore in spirit and truth sincere!
Glory and praise, O Bride of the Lord,
To thee the children of glory accord!

  What though the sons of darkness rebel,
Grating against thee the gates of Hell;
What though kings and princes unite
All their wisdom and all their might,
Leaguing together to do thee ill,
Leaguing to humble thee under their will;
Centred in Peter, still shalt thou see
An end of all that rise against thee!

  O happy kingdom, for ever to last!
O sweet shelter from misery's blast!

Offering to souls however distress'd,
However tempted, a refuge and rest!
Always to all the human race
A pillar of truth and fountain of grace!
Triumph of Jesus! bought with His Blood!
Thou hast the promises of our God.

   In thee I trust and wholly believe;
Thy words are His who cannot deceive.
Thee, whom Jesus loveth so well,
Deeper I love than words can tell!
Thee, whom the world hateth so sore,
For that very hatred I love thee more!
Thee in thy sufferings, thee in thy shame,
I praise, exult in, and honour the same,
As though already I saw thee array'd
In that high glory never to fade,
Predestined thine ere the worlds were made!

HYMN TO THE PRECIOUS BLOOD.

Neither with silver nor with gold
Were we redeem'd to God,
But by the Lamb without a stain
With his all-precious Blood.

O PRECIOUS Life-Blood of the Lord!
  In vain, with all our utmost thought,
We strive to estimate thy worth
  And glorify thee as we ought.

And must we then to Angels leave
  A task too high for mortal men,
A task exceeding all the powers
  Of human tongue or human pen?

Ah, no! To man by Thee redeem'd
  To man of right thy praise belongs,
And human words, by love inspired,
  May dare to vie with angel songs.

I praise Thee then, all-priceless Blood!
    I praise Thee, in thy height divine,
Subsisting in th' Eternal Word,
    United with th' Eternal Trine!

I praise Thee, by omniscient Love
    Predestined, ere the worlds began,
To be the life, redemption, bliss,
    Perfection, sanctity, of man.

I praise Thee, from creation's dawn.
    By type and prophecy foretold;
I praise Thee, the undying hope
    Of all the Patriarchs of old.

I praise Thee, Purity itself,
    From Adam's whole corruption free;
I praise Thee, of a Virgin sprung,
    Conceived Immaculate for Thee.

I praise Thee, shed in cruel pains
    To ransom us from Satan's thrall;
I praise Thee, offer'd on the Cross
    A perfect Sacrifice for all.

I praise Thee, in the Holy place;
    I praise Thee, at th' eternal throne,
Where our High Priest for ever pleads
    The price which He has paid alone.

I praise Thee, in the Sacred Heart
　　Which thy divine exultings thrill;
I praise Thee, on the Altar-stone
　　Within the Chalice offer'd still.

I praise Thee, the enduring Source
　　Of every saving grace below;
I praise Thee, in the Sacraments
　　Through which Thy living fountains flow.

I praise Thee, in the Church of God,
　　In all her works of faith and love;
I praise Thee in the souls elect,
　　I praise Thee in the Saints above.

O Precious Blood! may nought from Thee
　　The child of Thy Redemption part;
Still more and more be unto me
　　The life, the joy, which now Thou art!

⬥

THE HOLY MASS.

———

COULD it be so throughout the world,
   (Which Heavenly Grace forefend!),
That Mass and holy Priesthood
   Should find an utter end;

The Blood of Calvary once shed
   By pure redeeming Love,
Would still in Heaven be offer'd
   By our High Priest above;

But, oh! no more that Sacrifice,
   In all its boundless worth,
As now upon our Altars,
   Would cry for us from earth.

Ah, then, in absence of the grace
   Now flowing on mankind,
To what a hideous ruin
   The world would be consign'd!

THE HOLY MASS.

Into what darkness would it sink
    Without the strength to rise!
How would the burden gather
    Of its enormities!

Till no alternative remain'd
    But for the Judge to come,
And sound the final summons
    Of its eternal doom!

HYMN OF REPARATION TO THE MOST HOLY SACRAMENT.

O JESU! my Redeemer!
  How comforts it my heart
To meditate upon Thyself
  Here present as Thou art!

But with my joy there mingles
  A grief, to think again,
How many this high Gift deny,
  Or faithlessly profane.

Upon this Holy Altar,
  Beneath a form of Bread,
Dwells in eternal majesty
  Creation's Lord and Head!

And from the folds of darkness
  That veil His glory o'er,
I seem to hear Him pleading
  As from the Cross of yore.

" Come near," He says, " and be not
    So thankless and untrue;
For never suffer'd man so much,
    As I, your God, for you.

Come near, and in My presence
    A few short moments spend;
For quickly fleets your life away,
    And soon there comes an end;

But I, your dear Redeemer,
    Can endless pleasures give;
And whosoever comes to Me
    In Me shall ever live."

Thus from the Holy Altar
    Thou seemest, Lord, to plead;
But man, vain man, he passes on,
    And gives Thee little heed.

The world and its enticements
    His heart and mind engage;
On these he lavishes his youth,
    On these he spends his age!

O Christ, for all dishonours,
    Neglect, and cruel wrong,
Which Thou in this Thy Sacrament
    Sustainest all day long:

Accept this Reparation
    Unworthy though it be;
Accept the homage of my heart,
    Which here I offer Thee.

With all devout affections
    Enrich me from above;
That I may value as I ought
    This miracle of love;

With ever-growing ardour,
    May Thee in faith adore;
Until I see Thy face in bliss
    Unveil'd for evermore!

HYMNS FROM THE OFFICE OF REPARATION
TO THE MOST HOLY SACRAMENT.

VESPERS.

Quis dabit profunda nostro.

OH for perpetual sighs!
And floods of falling tears, to make lament
For all the profanations wrought against
 Our glorious Sacrament;
 For Heaven's own Pearl divine
 Trod under feet of swine!

 Still Herod makes pretence
Of adoration, and prepares to slay;
Still Judas gives his Lord the treacherous kiss
 Anew from day to day;
 Still bloody scourgings sore
 Rend Jesus as of yore.

The Father's Victim pure,
By His own people's savage outcry slain,
Now suffers in the Holy Eucharist
Grief from His own again,
Rejected by the pride
Of those for whom He died.

Come from on high, come down,
On wings of wrath, ye armies of the Lord!
And all who this His Marriage Feast refuse
Smite with avenging sword;
Who Marriage Robe have not,
In darkness be their lot.

Ah! but not so the Lamb
The gentle Lamb from this sweet Altar cries,
Who for His murderers embraced the Cross
And all its agonies:
With Judgment here He pleads,
For mercy intercedes.

Glory to Him whose love
Doth guilt's polluted vessels so endure;
Glory to Him whose sole redeeming Blood
Doth wash those vessels pure;
Praise to the Spirit rise
Who fits them for the skies!

MATINS.

Nunc Te flebilibus concinimus modis.

O THOU who art our glory and our bliss
    Here present with Thine own, Thyself their
        food,
To Thee our plaintive melody ascends,
    Most truly hidden God!

Alas! while Heaven its largesses outpours
    Against it in our madness we rebel,
Surpassing all the bounties of the Lord
    With greater deeds of Hell.

Ah! hath He so deserved? Hath He not given
    Freely to thee, O Vineyard, all He could?
For grapes He looks, and lo! a tangle wild
    Of worthless leaves and wood!

Here the blasphemer sits; here sacrilege
    Makes Jesus of its cruel fangs the prey;
Here worldliness intrudes with wandering mind,
    And empty goes away.

Oh, for the end! Come Truth, and all our clouds
    Disperse with radiance from thy Mount above;
Come down from Heaven, eternal Charity,
    And melt our hearts with love.

I.

Zeal for thine House by sinners so profaned
    Afflicts our souls, O gracious Trine and One:
Open to us that House by sin unstain'd,
    Where dwell the Saints alone!

LAUDS.

Novam ne das lucem Deus?

AND dost Thou grant another dawn,
    O Lord of glory blest?
Which sinners could not ask, nor they
    Could wish, who love Thee best!

Alas! how have we made ourselves
    For death and vengeance meet!
Alas for our Redemption's Blood
    Trod underneath our feet!

Oh, how for this with all our tears
    Can we enough atone,
The innocent for others' deeds,
    The guilty for their own!

Who could desire to live and see
    Thy Temples empty stand,
Or in their courts the Angels' Food
    By dogs of Hell profaned!

Far better that the newborn day
    Should sink in sudden night,
As once before at Calvary,
    Than show us such a sight!

Thou who alike on good and bad
    Dost make Thy sun to rise,
The harden'd rend, and stir Thine own
    To penitential sighs.

O Lamb of God for sinners slain,
    To Thee may purest praise
Amend for present injuries
    Through everlasting days.

AT TERCE AND THE OTHER HOURS.

O LAMB of God! who ever dost
    For sinners intercede,
All glory in the Trinity
    Be Thy eternal meed!

FLOWERS ON THE ALTAR OF THE BLESSED SACRAMENT.

A S on some ocean cliff
    Oft I have seen
A patch of flowers, along the perilous brink
    Basking serene

In blooming heedlessness,
    For all as though
No dread profundity of heaving main
    Upsurged below;

So by yon altar-flowers
    Glistening so fair
In their most delicate vases, each as in
    Its own parterre,

Opens a dread abyss,
    A sea immense,
Confounding in its dread reality
    All thought, all sense!

For there in hidden might
        Of glory dwells,
He who creation's whole infinitude
        So far excels,

    That countless worlds might blaze
        To nought, before
The fires of His magnificence, and all
        Would be no more,

    (If with His majesty
        We them compare,)
Than th' incense-wreath that round the altar
            rolls,
        Then melts in air!

HYMN FOR THE RENEWAL OF BAPTISMAL VOWS.

LOOK in pity, Lord of glory,
  On the suppliants at Thy feet;
Their baptismal vows renewing,
  Here before Thy mercy-seat.

SOLO.

By the sacred fontal waters
  Purer than the dew of morn,
In whose laver of salvation
  We to second life were born :—

CHORUS.

Satan and his pomps for ever
  Here we all renounce again ;
Here we promise, holy Saviour,
  Thine for ever to remain.

SOLO.

By the majesty unspoken
    Of the dread triunal Name,
In whose solemn invocation
    We the heirs of God became :—

CHORUS.

Satan and his pomps for ever, &c.

SOLO.

By the twofold solemn unction,
    Full of mysteries divine,
Consecrating us to Heaven
    In the Cross's awful Sign :—

CHORUS.

Satan and his pomps for ever, &c.

SOLO.

By the white baptismal raiment,
    Pledge of innocence regain'd,
To be borne before the presence
    Of the judgment-seat unstain'd :—

CHORUS.

Satan and his pomps for ever, &c.

MISCELLANEOUS PIECES.

SOLO.

By the mystic lighted taper
    Placed within our infant hands,
Ever to be brightly burning,
    Till in sight the Bridegroom stands;—

CHORUS.

Satan and his pomps for ever, &c.

ALL TOGETHER.

Lord and Saviour, God of mercy,
    Lord of lords, and King of kings;
Keep, oh, keep us now and always
    In the shadow of Thy wings.

As we chose at life's beginning
    Thee for our eternal Friend,
So in faith and love maintain us,
    Persevering to the end.

Mary, Joseph, Saints, and Angels,
    Intercede for us above;
From a wicked world's temptations
    Shield the children of your love;

Till with you in glory's kingdom
    We the song of glory sing
To the Father, Son, and Spirit,
    Your and our eternal King!

———————

ST. PHILIP NERI AND THE YOUNG NOBLE.

"UNHAPPY youth! so strangely vice
    Has dull'd thy spirit's finer sense,
That when I threaten endless Hell,
    My words appear a vain pretence.

We must to facts.   Come hither then :
    And kneeling here beside my knee,
Bend down thy face upon my lap,
    And for thyself behold and see!"

With easy grace, at Philip's feet
    The youthful noble knelt and gazed :
But, oh, another man was he
    When up again his face he raised!

" O Saint and Father, I repent,
    And here confess my guilt," he cries ;
" For what my heart had fear'd to own
    Has been before my very eyes!

I saw the hidden depth of Hell
    Disclosed in all its raging might;
I saw th' intolerable flames,
    And faint with horror at the sight!"

With tender strain St. Philip drew
    The frighted worldling to his breast,
And on his terror-stricken soul
    The truths of life eternal press'd.

Then all his saintly art he plied,
    Till fear in love had died away;
And so absolving sent him back
    Converted to his dying day!

HYMN TO ST. CHARLES BORROMEO.

Cœtus parentem Carolum.

O FATHER blest, and Founder!
 To thee our hearts we raise,
Rare pattern of a lovely life
 Above all human praise!

A glory o'er thy cradle
 The future Saint reveal'd,
Its little altars from the first
 Thy childhood loved to build.

Rome won in thee new honour,
 Her cardinal renown'd;
New life thy native Milanese
 In thee their Bishop found.

No longer, in thy presence,
 Their stormy factions rage;
Before thy firmness sink subdued
 The vices of an age.

In vain the leaden bullet
    Against thy breast is sped;
Before thee, like a rock, the shield
    Of thy dear God is spread.

Amidst the plague thou shinest
    An Angel of the Lord;
And so through all things conqueror
    Dost pass to thy reward;

Henceforward to the clergy
    A rule and model sure;
Hope of the flock; light of the world;
    And altar of the poor!

Oh, from thy glory hear us,
    Who sigh, dear Saint, to thee,
And present with us ever still
    In prayer and spirit be.

To th' everlasting Father
    All praise for evermore
Be with the Son and Holy Ghost
    As in all time before!

HYMN IN PRAISE OF ST. JOSEPH CALASANCTIUS.

Sacram venite supplices.

FLOCK hither, ye children, to-day,
    Round the altar of Joseph so blest;
Who first made the cause of poor children his own.
    And gather'd them all to his breast.

Ye Maidens, in jubilant hymns
    St. Joseph your Patron proclaim;
Who open'd a home for the perishing maid,
    To save her from peril and shame.

The poor and the sick, let them haste
    Of Joseph assistance to crave;
The poor he instructed, and fed in their need;
    And rescued the sick from the grave.

Let all on this day of his Feast
    The great Calasanctius praise;
His charity's ardour, his chastity's bloom
    Preserved from his earliest days.

Extol we his fortitude high,
  By which he resisted so well
The scorn of the world, and the fiery darts
  Sent forth from the quivers of Hell.

Extol we the gifts of his tongue;
  His labours and penance severe;
Oh, how can we all with devotion enough
  Our Parent and Founder revere?

All praise to the Father above;
  All praise to His infinite Son;
All praise to the infinite Spirit of love,
  While the days of Eternity run.

THE END.

LONDON:

ROBSON AND SON, GREAT NORTHERN PRINTING WORKS,
Pancras Road, N.W.

30 DE 64

ERRATA.

Page 123, last line but one, *for* foot *read* step

  „   184,   „   six, „ thee „   the

  „   148,   „   four, „ dread „ deep

www.ingramcontent.com/pod-product-compliance
Lightning Source LLC
Chambersburg PA
CBHW020232030726
47497CB00009B/3056